Synopsis

Will the nightmare ever end?

Murder in a beautiful English village and many secrets revealed.

A vicar, respected and loved by all his parishioners runs for his life with his young lover, leaving his wife, Daphne and daughter, Louise broken hearted.

The vicar's daughter, Louise, spirals into a world she doesn't understand and within a few years she is incarcerated for the murder of her married lover, Alex.

His wife Susannah left with a child to care for.

Daphne knows she has failed her daughter; consumed by the loss of her adulterous husband and the humiliation of his desertion she feels there is only one way out.

The village of Camberley Edge has many more messages for the discerning reader.

Law is a good master when disposed of fairly but cruel when not; as is life.

Acknowledgements

This is my first novel and has been the most difficult thing I have ever done. The story-line is fictitious and so are the characters but as an avid reader I like to learn something when I read. For that reason I have put effort into my research on several matters.

I would like to thank the following people.

Mr Alan Haskell who has given me help and advice regarding the gundogs in the story. The types of dogs used for hunting and their care.

Surinder Randhawa, Solicitor and colleague who was always at hand and ready to help throughout my endeavours, and debate any issues concerning law.

His Honour Judge Paul Thomas Q.C. who helped on points of law outside of my knowledge. I must admit to keeping some incorrect pieces vital to the story which I now call 'poetic licence', and take full responsibility. Judge Thomas was also kind enough to read an early manuscript of the book and gave me encouragement.

Mr Eilian Wyn Jones. Actor, writer, teacher to name just a few of his talents. It was he who taught me what I know and was brave enough to support me in the writing of this book by proof-reading and advising me, often. His expertise was invaluable.

As a wife, mother and grandmother it has been reassuring to have my family behind me. My husband, Noel, supports me in everything I do in life; I couldn't ask for more.

Introduction

Over the years, my work within the legal system has given me the opportunity to understand how the law in England and Wales works from the inside. The prosecution service and those who defend, seemingly working in opposition but ultimately in conjunction to ensure the law is seen to be fair.

Their clarity of representation in the courtroom is vital in order that the decision maker has everything needed to arrive at a fair and just conclusion. There can be no doubts.

Its sounds easy but we all know mistakes are sometimes made. Evidence which seems conclusive can change with the addition of further information unavailable at the time of judgement. You will see this throughout the plot.

So we begin to understand that there are many pieces to the puzzle. Putting the pieces together, in the correct way, is not easy.

Most cases in law are dealt with quickly, efficiently and accurately but on rare occasions things go wrong. The consequences of which can change lives.

Chapter 1

April 2016 – The Funeral

The tragedy of such an unexpected death reflected in the number of mourners. The church was full with some standing outside. It had stood in the centre of the small village for hundreds of years. It had seen beautiful, happy weddings, christenings and funerals of the older villagers who had enjoyed long lives. Today was very different. The years that had led up to this point had been cruel. Heartbreak and tragedy had left a young woman lost, confused and alone. Of course she knew it was her fault but the consequences of her actions had caused pain to so many.

It was to be expected that a seat in the church would be reserved for her. She waited patiently in the vehicle until all the mourners had taken their place; she then followed the coffin into the church and down the aisle. It seemed to take forever. When she reached the front she took her seat and sat alone. It was some time since she had sat in this church and she looked around strangely enjoying the familiarity. The surroundings gave her a little comfort and brought back happy memories of her early life in Camberley Edge; she had hoped that it would make this day more bearable; but sadly not.

The closed coffin was place at the front of the church, near the altar where her father had once stood every Sunday. There was a beautiful wreath of red roses and white orchids stretched across the length of the coffin lid. The mourners sat behind her and she could hear the hum of their incoherent whispers. Louise had hoped that her obvious grief and sadness would have softened the hearts of these people who had once been her friends, but they were strong in their conviction and treated her with the contempt that they believed she deserved.

The vicar took his place after stopping briefly in front of the coffin and nodding his head as a mark of his respect to the deceased. He welcomed the congregation on this sad occasion but he didn't look at Louise. Instead he looked down at the words he had prepared. You could hear the sadness in his soft voice as he spoke.

'Daphne was loved by all who knew her. Every day she thought of others, taking flowers to those who were ill, calling at the homes of the older members of our church to check how they were and often doing some shopping for them. Her energy and focus in doing the Lord's work was endless. A true Christian who will surely be with her Lord and Master in the Kingdom of Heaven. At times things were hard for Daphne but in the face of adversity she continued. When she needed help she took strength from the church fellowship and her faithful friends.' 'Something I rarely get the opportunity to say, but I can today. This is not simply a Christian funeral it's much more. It's the funeral of a true Christian. Let us pray for our friend Daphne.'

Before the first hymn was sung there was a murmuring from friends who knew it was Daphne's favourite; 'Blessed assurance, Jesus is mine'. Unusually, the Vicar read out the last verse instead of the first by means of an introduction. Everyone knew it had meaning for Daphne but no-one more than Louise, her only child.

'Perfect submission, all is at rest,

I in my Saviour am happy and blest;

Watching and waiting, looking above,

Filled with his goodness, lost in his love'

Louise stood as the church organist began to play. Her heart pounded in her chest and her hands shook as she tried to steady herself and stand up. She knew the words of the hymn by heart and tried to sing, but her legs gave way and she fell back onto her seat. No-one paid any attention to this young woman in distress; no-one cared. A feeling of nausea engulfed her and the sweat dripped from her head onto her raincoat. She didn't try to stand again, just sat and quietly wept, listening to the words being sung.

Louise longed to do the eulogy; she felt that there was so much to say. It had been thought inappropriate by the vicar and rightly so. Feelings were running high and there surely would have been a bad response. So instead of Louise, her mother's close friend for many years, Madge Johnson, spoke to the congregation about her best friend and the good life she had led.

But not a word of her daughter.

After the service Louise followed as the vicar led the coffin down the aisle and out of the great wooden door of the church. The bearers were all known to Louise. It was a short walk to the open grave in the corner of the church grounds but every step was such an effort for her. Again she stood alone; her red wavy hair was roughly tied back and buried beneath the upturned collar of her thin, brown raincoat. Jeans she used to fill to overflowing hung so loosely around her frame that the bottoms had slipped and were slowly drinking up the rain water from the muddy pool in which she stood. Her eyes were red from crying and her cheeks were so cold that she could feel the hot tears intersperse with the rain. So many tears, so much pain.

The vicar held an umbrella over himself and his Bible as he spoke softly to the gathering at the graveside; they watched the beautiful oak coffin being lowered into the ground. There were many tears shed that day. Louise had lost her mother; a mother who adored her and it seemed that the whole world blamed her for this dreadful mess.

So many familiar faces. Stern faces with just the odd sideways glance as Louise stood alone in the rain. They were people she had once known as friends, almost family. Today their faces showed hatred and contempt for her; they couldn't have made their feelings clearer. Some ignored her and one or two took pleasure in glaring at her. Yet, they all stood together as one, in silent respect. Louise searched the crowd for

Susannah but she wasn't there. Of course she wouldn't be, why would she? How she had grown to hate Susannah.

Looking from one ignoring face to another, Louise tried to find something, a little compassion, some sympathy. She saw her parents' good friends, Bob and Madge Johnson, who had always shown her love and affection; treating her as their own. She longed to run to them and have them hold her close one more time. As a child she would visit Madge often, or Auntie Madge as she called her, with her mother and on sunny summer days the women would sit in the garden drinking tea and Louise would play with Uncle Bob's Golden Retriever, Penny. Bob and Madge would have made great parents had they only been blessed. They didn't look her way.

Louise looked from one face to another. She spotted Edward Flint standing at the back of the crowd. He was a tall, proud man as a rule but today it seemed he was hiding amongst the mourners. He had no cause to do so. He'd done no wrong, but it was clear the shame that his daughter, Abigail, had brought upon him had taken its toll. Edward was a quiet man, a church goer, who had lost his wife to cancer. They had brought their daughter Abigail up well but as a teenager she'd made quite a name for herself when she'd developed a liking for boys, any boys, in the village and her reputation grew from there.

The committee for the annual village flower festival were out in force too. How would they manage without Daphne's dedication and commitment? She worked so hard for months before the festival with all the preparations, and the advertising drawing more crowds each year. Her own speciality would be her plants and flower arrangements. All lovingly grown in her greenhouse until they were ready for display, including her magnificent orchids.

Today Louise was an outcast. It seemed that the whole village had turned their back on the young woman they had known since she was born. They were so quick to judge. The pain and heartache she had caused her mother was unforgivable but there was no intent; all was done in child-like innocence. If anyone was to blame it was her dad, the Reverend George

7

Anderson. No matter now. It wasn't the time for excuses. It was the day that her dear mother was being laid to rest, alone.

Louise had so many thoughts running around in her confused mind, she wasn't coping with her situation and reached out for what she knew and understood. Thanks to her parents, her life as a child was spent with God in mind and she turned to him now.

'Please help me, God.' She mouthed the words in silence. 'Tell my mother I love her.'

The rain was getting heavier and the mourners became agitated as their feet sank into the sodden ground. The vicar spoke more quickly, raising his voice for all to hear. He looked around as he spoke and at last his gaze fell on the bedraggled Louise. Was he to be the one to show mercy? The Reverend David Green had known Louise for some time and she felt that as a man of God he should be more understanding, even forgiving. Grasping at straws, Louise smiled; there was no response from the young vicar. Her heart sank once more. He continued to speak, looking at the coffin.

'Daphne spent her life thinking and doing for others. Always a kind word, a helping hand to those in need. She leaves behind her only daughter Louise Georgina. May God have mercy upon Daphne, a wonderful woman who chose to leave this earthly world before You called for her, Lord.' That was the only time the mourners looked her way. A burning gaze, hot enough to singe her very soul. Her eyes pleaded with the faces that turned to her.

In desperation she cried out 'I loved her too,' not one of them responded. Louise bowed her head, not in shame but in despair. She took a handful of the earth offered to her and sprinkled it over the coffin deep in the ground as she whispered.

'I love you so much, Mum.' Louise's body ached with sadness; her heart was breaking. 'I will love you always.'

The firm, impatient hand on Louise's shoulder pulled at her tiny frame. She turned around abruptly and in front of everyone the handcuffs were secured around her wrists. The officers remained focussed and with measured actions that showed no pity or compassion. No more than a child at nineteen years of age, Louise had lost everything, her father, her mother, her lover and her freedom. It would have been so much easier if she was lying in the ground with her mother. Perhaps then the pain would end.

The male officer was tall, clean shaven with upper arms that forced the sleeves of his black, uniform jacket to swell and strain at the seams. One could only guess what lay beneath. His hat concealed his hair, if indeed he had any. He was wet through and seemed anxious to get out of the rain and return to the warmth of the vehicle awaiting them on the road outside the church grounds. The woman officer with him was short, fat and had yellow hair sticking out in all directions beneath her hat; she seemed uncertain of what to do and obeyed his every command. They chatted to each other but never to Louise. It was a short walk to the van and the officers held firmly onto Louise's shackled arms as they marched her over the mud and stones to the church gate, then across a busy road towards the waiting vehicle and driver. Louise didn't know if it was the rain in her eyes or the burning tears that never ceased but she could hardly see where she was going. As they got closer to the waiting van she felt her heart sink with despair at what was awaiting her back at the prison. Her legs could no longer support her and her body shook, yet again more tears; she seemed to have no control over her emotions. Her reasons for caring left her and she became a lost soul. All she wanted was to be with her mother, safe and warm in her loving arms.

Louise stopped and turned just before getting into the van. She took one final look behind as she left her mother for the last time. They were all watching her now.

'She has a nerve to come here today,' others nodded agreement. 'She should rot in that prison cell for what she's done.' The remarks were said loudly and clearly for her to hear every word.

'Dear God' she screamed back at them 'How much more can I take?'

9

The woman pushed her roughly into the van. 'Shut up or you'll be in even more trouble! Now get in.'

Perhaps it was for the best that Louise didn't know what the future held for her.

Chapter 2

Early Life in Camberley Edge.

Louise's childhood had been idyllic in many ways and had afforded her many wonderful memories. In the lonely darkness of her prison cell when sleep was hard to find, a smile would be a comforting friend as she remembered the good, happy times. A wonderful childhood growing up in Camberley Edge and living in the vicarage with her mother and father. As with most vicarages it was big; not only many rooms but many big rooms all painted in bold, classical colours with heavy drapes dressing the large windows. The garden was beautiful, especially in summer. There were old trees that had probably stood before the house had been built, now tall and strong; some even bearing fruit. One in particular offered many kilos of sweet red apples each year. Bedding plants of all colours and sizes adorned the borders, courtesy of her green fingered mum.

Her dad had created a little girl's dream; a play area with a double swing and a slide. Animal-shaped bouncy things that rocked when you sat on them; you had to hold on for your life but she often fell off onto the thick green lawn that her dad mowed weekly. The garden pond was magical. There were no expensive coy carp but hundreds of tadpoles in the spring which later turned their garden into a moving carpet of leaping frogs. It was a mystery to Louise when, somehow, they would disappear all at once leaving behind the next generation of tadpoles as dormant spawn floating on the murky waters of the large pond.

Louise's favourite, her pride and joy, was an old garden shed that her father had painted pillar box red and her mother had made lace curtains for the window. Inside there was an old arm chair with a crocheted blanket as a throw, a small plastic table with a gingham table cloth and four chairs. There was also a floral china tea set that her mother had once owned as a little girl. Louise played house with her friends all through the summer months, lost in a world of make believe.

All through her childhood, Louise had been popular at school and often brought her friends home for tea, always surprising her mother with unexpected guests. Born and raised in the village and an only, treasured, child of parents who were devoted to her. Some would say she was spoilt. It was a fact that Louise was a normal, happy child cocooned by her adoring mother and father. She remembered every day of her childhood with love and affection knowing that she was just the luckiest girl in the world. How could things have gone so badly wrong?

Nothing could take those precious, happy memories away from her and she would relive the good times over and over in her head each and every night. In real terms, life at the vicarage had changed in a flash and Louise's fairytale life was snatched cruelly away at the age of fourteen. Her father, the Reverend George Anderson, destroyed everything they held precious when he left them for that woman, seemingly out of the blue. Louise and her mother had certainly not seen it coming. Their life together was good, as far as she was concerned; what had she missed? Nothing had seemed to change in any way. There had been no tell-tale signs before the departure of George and there had certainly been no clues as to what was to come. As usual Daphne was happily supporting George, as was her expected role as the wife of the vicar. The parish and its parishioners were always his priority, and rightly so, but over the years Daphne was becoming more involved with the festival committee and managing of the annual village flower festival.

George was pleased to see Daphne doing something for herself for a change and it was clear that she enjoyed every minute of it. Family time together had seemed normal to Louise. Her dad had even erected a superb greenhouse in the garden for his green fingered wife to develop her love of orchid growing, amongst other things. How could it all have just fallen apart so unexpectedly?

The physical pain of losing her dad was never far away and the agony as she watched her mother suffer, grieved the young Louise. They shared each other's pain which slowly manifested itself in an all consuming hatred for George; a hatred beyond words. A hatred which grew and festered each and every lonely day and night, enveloping their every thought. It was a betrayal that would never have been expected of a vicar, least of all the doting father. A pillar of the community of Camberley Edge for many years, a good man, above the weaknesses of the flesh. Or so they all had mistakenly believed.

They had both been deserted by the man who was supposed to love and care for them and they were left devastated in the wake of his confession. It became a struggle to get on with their daily lives. They went through the motions of living but lost the spring in their steps and the sparkle in their eyes. Louise was the more vulnerable one, taking the desertion much harder than anyone realised. At only fourteen years of age the desperate feeling of rejection by her father's desertion broke her spirit. Daphne tried hard to mend the damage to her little girl but sometimes the demands on her time and her own emotions overshadowed the unseen psychological needs of her daughter. Louise wasn't doing well; she had begun to sink further and further into a place of darkness. A spiral that was spinning out of control leading to a paranoia of loathing and self hatred with the belief that her father's desertion was more about leaving her, than his moving on with someone new. Her desire to be loved became obsessive. It was to be her downfall. Louise was lost.

Night after lonely night in her prison cell Louise would weep with sadness and regret as she remembered the wasted evenings when mother and daughter would remind themselves how much he had hurt them both. They'd talk together until the early hours about how they'd reject him the day he came crawling back, begging for forgiveness. Sharing their bitterness and sinking into a pattern of manifest darkness.

As she had grown into her teenage years, Louise knew only too well that she hadn't inherited her mother's good looks. Daphne was an attractive woman with blonde hair that framed a heart-shaped, flawless face with natural soft curls; she could have been a movie star. Her deep blue eyes were large and appealing; she had an hourglass figure with sensual curves. Had she not been the wife of the vicar she could have been quite a

13

temptress but that would never have crossed Daphne's mind; George was her reason for living. Louise smiled as she remembered her beautiful mother. Daphne seemed unaware of her own beauty and vibrant personality but at the same time it seemed to subconsciously give her the confidence needed to be a good vicar's wife. She had the ability to step back and take second place to her husband, to be an active partner to a man who was adored, even favoured by his parishioners.

Louise, on the other hand, was the female double of her father. What was a fitting image for George, some would say even handsome, was not a particularly feminine look for a growing girl. In her favour, Louise was a sweet young thing; innocent, popular and bright. If she had learned anything from her father's desertion it was to rely only on herself and not depend on others. She worked hard and was doing well with her GCSEs fast approaching. She simply had to remain focused but this was to become more difficult.

Daphne made efforts to compensate for George walking out on them; always trying to rebuild Louise's confidence by telling her how well she did things. What a successful young lady she could be if she worked hard at school! These words were well-meant and said with love but it would soon become apparent that the damage was deep and irreparable. Daphne would wear a cheerful façade and try her best to lighten the conversation after dinner but it inevitably turned to George. The pair were hopelessly spinning and falling into a pattern of inescapable self-destruction and no one even noticed. It had to stop.

Louise tried to remember when exactly her mother turned their lives around and started looking to the future. Somewhere along the way Daphne became busier. It was a slow start but she began to commit herself more to village life. She started by joining every committee she could and, most importantly after being a housewife since the day she married George, she decided to look for a job to support the two of them and give them independence and respect. There was an opportunity at the local post office, a position that she fell into perfectly and relished. Suddenly there was a life to be had without George and Daphne began feeling happy for the first time in a long while.

Before marrying George, Daphne had worked for a local accountancy firm and had always had a good head for figures. The post office was the ideal place for her. It was the hub of the village. A meeting place for the gossips who shared the scandal and the daily news; not that there was much in a sleepy village like Camberley Edge. Not only was it a post office, it was also a general store that sold everything from birthday gifts and newspapers to daily fresh bread. Daphne's friend Madge, the owner, tried to cater to everyone's needs; there were even a few tables where you could sit and have a cup of tea. Pension day was chaos.

Madge and her husband Bob had run the post office for years and were good friends to Daphne. They encouraged her to rebuild a new life for herself and Louise. Madge and Bob had grown up in Camberley Edge just like Daphne and George. Daphne and Bob had worked together at L & J Thomas Associates, the only accountancy firm in the village or for miles around for that matter. The two couples married about the same time but Madge and Bob were never blessed with children. Instead they developed the small post office and made a good living for themselves. George's leaving was a shock to all that knew him and Madge became a pillar of support for her friend, Daphne.

Madge was always trying to convince Daphne that at only forty one years of age there may be a chance that she could remarry and start again with someone who would love and value her. There may be someone out there who could turn her life around and make her happy again. After all, she had the looks and personality. No-one could understand why George had left her in the first place; they seemed so content together. The two had been childhood sweethearts and everyone in the village had watched their relationship develop into the perfect couple. Childhood sweethearts and so in love. When George proposed to her the news circulated the village in no time and their wedding was a very public affair.

George Anderson was a well-respected man of the cloth and considered himself fortunate to eventually become the vicar of the parish he knew so well, Daphne had supported him through Theology College and was prepared to follow him to the ends of the earth. It was divine intervention, Daphne used to say, that God had chosen them to work in the parish they loved so much.

The church and vicarage were in the centre of the village and there were always people calling in. As a toddler Louise thought it was quite normal to come home from school to find visitors in the parlour with her dad. From an early age she had learned that when the parlour door was closed and there were voices from within, she had to be quiet.

Daphne had willingly relinquished her position in the local accountancy firm to become a full time vicar's wife and eventually mother to baby Louise. Sadly the couple lost both sets of parents within a five year period and before Louise was born so they never got to see or hold their lovely granddaughter. George and Daphne drew on their faith to give them strength and their friends for practical support. Life went on. The church was central to life in the village and there was something on in either the church or the church hall every day, George and Daphne's role in the village was pivotal and they were just made for it.

Louise Georgina was born and named after her dad, George. She grew up looking so much like him. Both were tall with red hair, a ghostly white complexion and prominent teeth which dominated their smile. Louise adored her dad and he worshipped her.

As a teenager she didn't particularly like her middle name, Georgina, and when George left she hated the fact that her name would always be a reminder of her Dad.

Daphne thought things could only get better; she was so wrong.

Chapter 3

February 2016 - The Trial

Daphne's fall into depression started when Louise was first arrested and it soon became apparent that her mother was not coping; but just how seriously ill and mentally unstable she really was didn't become obvious for quite a while. Daphne did and said uncharacteristic things. On more than one occasion she went to the small police station in the village and begged them to free her daughter saying that she would go to prison in her place.

'Take me! It was me! Lock me up!' She tried to tell the officers in the police station. Her words were mumbled and sometime incoherent due to the drugs she had been prescribed. This behaviour was forming a pattern and an officer would just escort her safely home. She'd walk the streets of the village after dark and knock on doors until the occupant answered. She'd tell them she needed their help to get her daughter out of jail; most knew her and would take her in for a cup of tea until she calmed herself and went home. Daphne's best friend, Madge, would spend hours trying to console her but eventually everyone realised she needed expert help in the form of a psychiatric consultant. After a few consultations it had been decided that increased medication and home care would help Daphne in the interim. There was no way she would be allowed to see her daughter whist on remand or attend court for her trial; her understanding of the situation was confused and her consultant thought it wiser to keep the details away from her until matters were more settled. The drugs she was given took away Daphne's ability to question and she became content in her ignorance; just like a child.

Because of the charge of murder against Louise and the inevitable sentence if convicted it became clear that she would certainly be remanded in custody. The remand wing of a prison where defendants await their trial or sentencing is less intensive in comparison to the other prison wings. Louise was just eighteen and had a vulnerable nature but her fate was to be the same as others on the wing with no special consideration.

Christmas Day, 2015, came and went with little importance paid other that a turkey lunch with a Christmas cracker. The time dragged for Louise in prison and the constant barrage of questions from her advocate each week as he prepared her defence seemed endless. Suddenly, the day had arrived and she was taken in a secure vehicle to The Crown Court where the trial would be heard.

Everything had been explained to Louise regarding the process and the formality of the court. But it was still a terrifying experience. The barrister for the Crown Prosecution Service was a tall gentleman with rimless glasses which sat precariously on the end of his nose. His voice was loud and he spoke with slow clarity and depth. When he put his case for The Crown he addressed the jury, looking at them intently one by one and without moving his gaze from the twelve men and women who would decide Louise's fate. From time to time he would point dramatically to the frightened Louise, but never took his stare away from the jury. The atmosphere was intense and his words well rehearsed.

The legal aid solicitor sat in the courtroom behind the appointed barrister for her defence. They had only spoken for half an hour before the court rose but the experienced barrister, an expert in his field and a Q.C. had assured Louise he would do his utmost to convince the jury of her innocence. His words had comforted the young girl, but what he actually meant was he intended to prey on their sympathy for a love-struck young woman with no experience of life. There were no witnesses for the defence as her mother had been deemed unreliable and liable to make matters worse. There was little or nothing to offer in mitigation.

It wasn't easy for Louise to follow the jargon of the proceedings. She felt lost and alone. The trial continued.

It was now her turn to be called to the witness box in her own defence. She wasn't considered a flight risk but security kept an eye on her all the same. She stood trembling as she read the oath. The judge was a big man with a beard and booming voice but he showed Louise some compassion by inviting her to sit for the questioning. She was grateful.

The judge could see that Louise was becoming distressed. He offered her a glass of water which the court usher promptly handed to her. Louise couldn't stop her hand from shaking and the usher helped her to take a drink.

'Would you like to take a comfort break, Miss Anderson?' The judge asked in a measured voice.

'No thank you sir, I'm fine.'

The trial continued.

Louise looked at the faces of the jurors and they stared back. She wondered what they were thinking. There was no-one in the viewing gallery but there was a solitary man sitting at the side of the court making notes. She realised he was from the press.

Her barrister was gentle and encouraged Louise to speak freely. He guided her through the events of the evening in question and she began to feel a little more relaxed.

Then came the time for the prosecution barrister to rise. Louise knew he would have to cross examine her and she took a deep breath thinking how silly he looked in those rimless glasses that sat on the end of his nose. He looked at her for what seemed like minutes before he spoke. He looked down at his notes and began. It seemed to start well. Firstly he engaged in a kindly duologue which put Louise at her ease. She was comfortable and fell into the false security of his well- practiced and well-rehearsed sophism that had been honed to perfection over the years. Mr Grey Q.C. was an artist at work. His questions were almost banal. He created a sense of calmness which relaxed her need for defence. Perhaps she had misjudged him when he gave his address at the beginning of proceedings. Maybe he was fair and just and she was warming to his glasses.

'In my role as prosecutor it is really not my job to persecute you Miss Anderson, simply to find the truth and explore the facts so that these good people,' he took a breath and gestured to the jury with a dramatic swing of his long arm, 'can make the true and correct decision,' his face contorted, 'and we all know what that is. Don't we?' Louise was taken back with his change of character. She was right the first time he was a nasty bit of work. But good, frighteningly good.

Louise felt an ache in the pit of her stomach as the barrister asked her about her and Alex's clandestine meetings when his wife was at work.

'Did you spend time in your lover's home, Miss Anderson?'

She nodded.

'Speak up for the jury to hear you please.' The barrister demanded.

'Yes.'

'Would you say you were there at every opportunity?'

'Yes.' Louise answered.

'Would you say you had become besotted by this man and had become reliant on his attention?'

The defence barrister began to rise but the judge waved him down, anticipating his objection.

'Do not lead the witness, Mr Grey.' Said the judge firmly and nodded to the prosecution barrister to continue.

'I imagine it must have been hard for you, Miss Anderson; keeping a secret of your love for Alex Turner. Tell me; were you jealous of his wife?'

As Louise sat in the dock, her tears told their own story.

The barrister continued. 'No more questions, Your Honour,' He raised his arm and gestured to Louise as he looked at the jury. He sat down.

The time had come for the final summing up. This was long and repetitive on both sides. A symphony of words, legal jargon and utter boredom. Louise hardly recognised herself in the story telling.

Then it was over. The jury filtered out through their own door to whatever lay beyond and Louise was taken down into the court cells where she was given a sandwich and cup of tea. Her solicitor joined her and explained what would happen next. It came more quickly than either of them thought. They were summoned back to the courtroom. Her advocate didn't smile but touched her shoulder gently. He left and took his place in the courtroom. Louise followed.

The jury marched in one my one and took their seats.

'Will the foreman of the jury please stand?' Louise didn't know where the voice giving the instructions came from but the man on the end of the front row of the jury stood. He glanced at Louise briefly.

Louise was standing in the dock directly opposite the judge but lowered her gaze saying a silent prayer.

That voice again. 'Sir, has the jury come to a decision?'

'Yes, we have.' Was the short response.

'And how to do find the defendant. Guilty or not guilty of the charge of murder?'

'We find the defendant.' he hesitated for a second which seemed like for ever. 'Guilty.'

Louise fell to her knees but was quickly pulled to her feet by the two guards and held firmly.

Her barrister got to his feet and addressed the judge in mitigation.

'Your Honour. Louise has no criminal record. It is clear that her emotions controlled the situation and she was unable to make responsible decisions. I ask that you consider that she was unable to deal with the information that her lover's wife had become pregnant when she believed she had a future with him. It seems she was led by Alex Turner for his own gain. Although Louise pleaded not guilty to the murder and is therefore not entitled to a reduction in sentence, I would ask for clemency due to her age and inexperience of life.'

The Crown Court Prosecutor, Mr Grey stood to point out the aggravating factors. Which he did exceedingly well.

The judge spoke.

'Miss Anderson. Please stand. You have heard the decision made by the jury and I see no purpose in prolonging this case for consideration as to sentence. I have listened to the mitigation put forward by your barrister today but you have shown no remorse for your actions and the heartbreak caused to the family of Alex Turner. It is clear to me that the sentence must be one of a considerable term of custody. So, for the wilful murder of Alex Rhydian Turner you will serve a term of imprisonment. A life sentence which will be for no less that fifteen years.'

The pronouncement was brief and succinct. Louise was helped back to the court cells to await transport back to H.M.P. Lockwood Park.

Chapter 4

Louise Begins Her Custodial Sentence.

After being sentenced Louise was returned to Lockwood Park. The ordeal of registration and security distressed her but she had to comply. She was then relocated to a secure wing for long serving prisoners.

The secure wing is very different to the remand wing. As its name suggests, the remand wing is where Louise was remanded in custody awaiting trial. It holds alleged offenders who may be found not guilty at trial. Their human rights have to be protected and, although they are locked up, they have freedom within that wing. They are allowed to wear clothes of choice and have many privileges that convicted prisoners do not have.

The others, who are found guilty at trial, move on to an appropriate wing for their crime.

The female prisoners incarcerated long term were all either dangerous or crazy. Maybe not totally mad but extreme and unusual characters. They were there because they had committed a serious crime, such as murder, and were proven to be a danger to society. There is always hope that with the programmes available to them they would be rehabilitated in some way, although few rarely were.

Louise had no idea what was in store for her on the secure wing but she soon found out when she met Tracy. This woman was beyond understanding and a cruel choice as a cell partner for Louise. Tracy ignored Louise's presence when she walked in that first day and continued to lie on her bed smoking. Within a few days Louise realised this was her future until one of them either walked free or was moved to another cell. Tracy continued to smoke heavily and intimidated Louise at every opportunity.

After a while Louise began to realise that most of the other inmates on that wing were the same. Fights broke out often and only rarely were the correct offenders punished for the disturbance. There were only a few who ever spoke to Louise during association. Staring and whispering was common when a newcomer arrived.

Most of the women looked forward to socialising early evening in a small area where there were chairs and tables on the wider part of the landing. Louise found it difficult to know how to deal with situations that cropped up. There were fights between the prisoners who tried to claim power. Louise wanted to speak up and tell the guards the truth about who really started it but she was soon told to back off and mind her own business. If she got involved she would get hurt herself.

The day to day regime of the wing was made clear to her from the start. There would be chores, plenty of them. Louise was told that she had to mop the floor of the entire wing and cells daily. Attention to detail was paramount as they would be inspected afterwards. Once a week they would be polished by another inmate. Others would help in the kitchens, collect trays and rubbish, distribute reading books and many other tasks.

Louise had never given a thought to the fact that she would have to work in the prison. It kept her busy so she didn't mind. She was also told that some of the jobs carried a small salary; she was eager to find out which ones.

As the weeks went by she began to see that there were a few women she could trust and sat with them during association.

It was when she was sitting there one day that a guard addressed her.

'The Governor wants a word with you Anderson. Come with me.'

Louise was directed to a small office near the double gates at the far end of the wing.

When she entered the Governor told her to sit. She obeyed.

'I've got some bad news for you Anderson. Your mother has committed suicide at your home; overdose I believe.'

He let a moment pass for Louise to absorb the information then continued.

'You will be informed of the date of the funeral and you can fill in this form,' he held a sheet of paper out for her to take. 'It's an application for you to attend the funeral. You don't have to go if you don't want to. The choice is yours.'

He got up and left the room. Louise was taken back to her cell where she lay on her bed for the whole afternoon trying to cry.

Chapter 5

April 2016   -   The Journey back after the funeral.

The day of the funeral had been the worst. It all seemed like a horrible dream. Not one person offered a hand in compassion. Everything about life had changed for Louise. Now that her mother had been laid to rest there was nothing left. It had been made all too clear, by their absence in court, that Louise had no friends and wasn't wanted in the village. It broke her heart. The journey back to HMP Lockwood Park after the funeral seemed to be the beginning of the end. The end of her life as she had known it; with no future to look forward to. Even though her mother had not been able to support her through the trial Louise had hope that her beloved mother would recover and maybe even visit her in prison. She had faith that her mother would be the one to believe her and take her side. She prayed for her mother every single night. People recovered from mental breakdowns and she believed her mother would be one of the survivors.

The aching sobs slowly ebbed away as she sat in silence in the back of the van. All she felt was exhaustion and despair. Where was her God now? It was a strange and unreal feeling for Louise to question her own faith but for just a short moment she did.

The male guard sat in the front with the woman who drove the van and chatted but from the back it was just an unintelligible mumble. The female guard was given the job of sitting with Louise; they sat opposite each other as the seats went from back to front on either side. The windows were dark so that no-one could see in and there was a protective glass partition behind the driver separating the front from the back seats. The glass partition was threaded with some kind of mesh, probably needed if a prisoner got violent or tried to escape. Louise had no intention of doing either. The double doors that secured the back of the van were locked from the outside but there was also an inner metal door that was locked independently, again for security.

The journey would take a few hours depending on traffic and Louise was not looking forward to sitting opposite that woman for any length of time. Her appearance was a little strange; her hair was bright blonde with a yellow tinge. Now that she had taken off her hat for the journey, Louise could see that her natural colour was dark brown. Well that was the colour of her roots. She had on a little makeup but the pathetic attempt to improve her appearance certainly didn't work. The rain during the interment caused the guards' mascara to spread around her eyes like a panda and she didn't even know. Her uniform was far too tight as if it had been handed down to her from a slimmer officer. Her tummy hung over the black leather belt supporting her black, baggy trousers. The plump layers around her middle forced her to sit upright and added to the strangeness of her whole appearance.

As had become usual over the past few months, Louise would lose herself in thought; a world of her own. She sat in silence with her blonde keeper. Her thoughts enticing her into a game of questions and wonder. How would she cope with her incarceration? What would she do when she got out? It was clear that she could never go home and there would be nothing to go home to anyway. There was a mortgage on the house and with no payments being made it would surely be repossessed; there would be little or no equity if it were to be sold. Things couldn't get any worse and thinking about the whys and wherefores wasn't helping.

There was no-one now. No-one to help her or even care a little. She would be thirty four years of age, if she was lucky, on release and an eternity on licence. She smiled at the way she had picked up the terminology of the prison. Although she knew the words, it hadn't been made clear what 'licence' meant. She made a mental note to ask someone on the wing when she got back; they'd know.

Louise slid across the seat as the woman driving the van swerved taking a corner too fast.

Her dad would have said 'Woman drivers, always going too fast.' It wasn't true of all woman drivers as he well knew, but he'd say it to annoy her mum and she fell for it every time. It always ended in laughter. How she longed for those days when life was good and happiness blessed her family.

There were obscenities coming from the driver and she heard the words 'Dammed cyclist.' She listened as the rhythm of the windscreen wipers increased to cope with the heavy rain. And the journey continued.

It wasn't an easy journey, mostly cross-country with no motorway or even dual carriageway available on that route. There was a lot of unexpected bouncing around going on in the back which wasn't a pretty sight for Louise with Miss Piggy in her direct line of sight. At one point the officer even suggested to the driver that speed was not conducive to a safe journey; or words to that effect. It had no effect and the front seat passengers continued to chatter to each other which seemed to upset Louise's companion.

'Are you new to Lockwood Park Miss?' Louise ventured to make some light conversation.

'No.' was the curt response. Louise gave up and tried to look through the darkened windows at the passing scenery. Too fast around another bend and Louise slid down the bench seat crashing against the inner door at the back of the van.

'Take it easy Jan. We'll be killing the prisoner at this rate.' Miss Piggy laughed as she pulled Louise back to the middle of the bench. There was shouting from outside the van as the wheels splashed gutter rain into a group of pedestrians waiting to cross the road. The officer shook her head in despair.

Before getting into the van Louise had noticed that it was unmarked. Perhaps it was procedure to use unidentifiable vehicles for such occasions, she thought. It wasn't the usual type of prison transport vehicle; they were much larger with clear markings on the outside and owned by private companies rather that the prison service. Louise remembered the one that took her from the courthouse to Lockwood Park. The steps were steep to climb into the vehicle and there were rows of small cubicles on either side with a passage from back to front. Each cubicle was locked separately and begs the question of how a prisoner would get out if there had been an accident and the vehicle rolled over. Apparently the roof would open in an accident and as the prisoners weren't handcuffed inside the cubicles, they could climb out. Louise remembered the moulded yellow seats in each cubicle and how hard they were to sit on. They were also extremely small and so uncomfortable for long journeys. Her knees touched the front panel as she sat down and she had red marks to prove her discomfort. Security was obviously the priority and not comfort.

Although Louise was probably not considered a flight risk, statistics have it that most escapes occur when prisoners are in transit; either from prison to court or days like these.

Time passed slowly and day light was fading. The man in the front shouted to the officer with me.

'Get ready, we've about a mile to go.'

Louise heard him speak to someone on his mobile phone. He told them they were a mile away so she presumed it was the prison. Stiff after sitting so uncomfortably for such a long time she stretched her legs and back. The van stopped outside the prison gates and they were all identified by the oversized security officers who never smiled. The driver drove through and stopped at the main entrance. The loud hiss of the electronic security gates could be heard as they locked behind the vehicle.

Chapter 6

March 2011 – Georges' Affair with Abigail Flint

Louise was fourteen years old and becoming more like her father each day. At five foot nine inches she was taller than most of her friends and only two inches shorter than her dad. Daphne adored her only child. They'd fall into heaps of laughter when they both said the same thing at the same time almost as if they shared each others thoughts. After dinner, Daphne would wash the dishes and Louise dry; George would disappear into the parlour and work on his sermon for the coming Sunday, that is unless he had some pastoral visits which could take him away from home for hours. He seemed to have a lot of those lately. The family rarely watched television, but Daphne and Louise would often sit and chat about Louise's day and her subjects at school; the light hearted chatter mostly turned into Daphne helping with her homework, especially her maths.

Louise would laugh and say, 'For a mum you're not so bad, in fact quite handy to have about.' Daphne was very good at mathematics and more than pleased to help. From the day she was born Louise had been her priority and never far from her thoughts. Daphne wanted everything good for her daughter and often wished she had given her the gift of siblings. Sadly that wasn't to be, so she gave more of herself to compensate. Louise was indeed the most precious, long awaited only child of a couple who had set up home together as newlyweds. George and Daphne knew the village well as they had grown up there and felt blessed that George had been given it as his first post as vicar of the parish of Camberley Edge, Hertfordshire where they were known and loved. Their dream had always been to have a child as soon as possible but it had taken longer than they had expected. Their dear friends Bob and Madge had experienced the same problems. Years passed before Daphne gave birth to Louise but Madge never did have any luck in conceiving.

As a child Louise was a little shy outside her home and, as most only children, had learned to be content with her own company. When she went to primary school she blossomed, making friends by the dozen. The teachers had their work cut out with Louise at first; when she wanted a toy or game she took it. Sharing was difficult for the only child, probably because she had everything to herself at home. The teachers at her school knew exactly how to deal with these matters and Louise became the perfect pupil with the correct type of discipline which she seemed to lack at home. The vicarage was a large family home so there were many unused rooms and Louise played in them all, especially in the winter months when it was too cold to play outside. She brought a different friend home each night and loved showing them around her home. Her bedroom was idyllic, decorated in lilac and pink. The bed was a mini four poster with net drapes all around for effect and many fluffy toys lying on the bed, even at night, when she snuggled in between them. The small wardrobe was full of pretty dresses and she had more shoes than many women. There were hooks in the ceiling from which all sorts of decorations hung. A large lilac butterfly hanging from a long elastic string was Louise's favourite; it would move and sway when her window was open and there was a breeze from outside. At night, the soft glow from her night light would sit gently on the silver glitter at the tip of its wings and she'd dream her way to fairyland as she drifted off to sleep. Another of her favourite ceiling hanging toys was a small colourful plastic parrot in a wooden cage that made weird sounds when there was movement in the room. It had been a gift from Auntie Madge and Uncle Bob from one of their exotic holidays. Her parents doted on her, calling her their little princess and Louise acted the part. Whether they wanted more children was never mentioned outside of their relationship but it was presumed by one and all that they chose to dedicate their lives to Louise, their everything. Little did they know how much Daphne wanted more children and her personal pain when it never happened.

The Reverend George Anderson always seemed a good husband and father, as was expected of a man of the cloth. No-one even noticed George's increasing interest in Abigail Flint, probably because of her age. It was common practice for George to give care and time to those who needed him, his pastoral duties always came first and Daphne understood completely. In fact she encouraged him.

Abigail was more than twenty years his junior and in comparison to Daphne, quite flamboyant in a common sort of way. Again, this young woman was brought up well with good parents but had earned the reputation, from a young age, of being free with her affections in regards to the opposite sex. All through her early school years she was just a pretty little girl with pigtails, and then as she reached puberty she discovered boys and developed physical advantages over girls with less noticeable attributes as she. Abigail Flint had undoubtedly become the best looking girl in the school and lapped up the attention and advantages this afforded her. Pubescent boys fawned over her, drooling as their unhidden gaze failed to raise itself above the firm large breasts which seemed to have a life of their own and for some reason seemed always to be on display. Some would say fair game. These young men became besotted by Abigail and fell under her spell with a serious view to progressing a relationship, not that they really understood what that meant. The words love and marriage were often used and Abigail, in innocence, believed every word they said. And so the cycle went on. The sexual attention she received alienated her from the girls, especially when she stole their boyfriends. Her friends stopped meeting up with her in the evenings and she became isolated. Even with all the attention she got from boys, she was fast becoming a very lonely soul.

Mrs Flint, Abigail's mum, was an attractive lady herself and wanted her daughter to have the best things in life, sparing no expense especially when Abi wanted a new dress for a party; she also advised her on make up to accentuate her already beautiful features. Perhaps, deep down, Abi wanted to be one of the girls but didn't know how to recapture the friendships; it certainly didn't help that she always ended up with one or more of their boyfriends.

At nineteen years old and only five years older than Louise, Abi was a woman and knew what men wanted from her. The type of men she attracted were certainly not interested in her mind, no matter what they said. Her long, slim legs seemed to go on forever. She was tall, around five foot eight inches and always wore high heels which added a few inches more to her height, sometimes even taking her over six foot. George was slightly shorter when Abi had on her best shoes; they were an improbable couple in so many ways.

Even George didn't understand how it all happened. To begin with he just visited to pray with the whole family when Abi's mother had been diagnosed with terminal cancer. Edward Flint would be at work during the day, so George mostly called early evening before Abigail left for her job at the village pub. It was always his intention to be of support to them all in their time of need. When Abi's mum was so poorly that she didn't even recognise her own daughter, George could see how badly Abigail was affected and as he left he would give her a fatherly hug; he felt that was entirely appropriate under such conditions.

Mrs Flint's premature death hadn't come easy for her husband, Edward, and Abigail; she had been diagnosed with renal cancer at the stage when there was little to be done. The cancer travelled to her liver and ended up going to her brain which was extremely distressing to watch; she became aggressive to those near her which affected Abi deeply. The only thing to be done was make her as comfortable possible, with the help of daily nursing at home but Abi was young to be dealing with the things she had to do for her mother. When Elizabeth Flint was lucid she had asked both her husband and daughter not to let her die in hospital; neither realised at that time what it entailed but they couldn't refuse her last wish. It was a struggle for them both.

The thought of losing a mother at such a young age was too much to bear for Abigail. Then after her mum passed away George helped with the funeral arrangements and continued calling at the Flint family home; just as he did with all his parishioners.

George began to look forward to the visits which moved from evenings to daytime when Edward was at work. Abigail looked forward to seeing George and listening to his words of kindness, in fact she relied on it. Some might have said she had become a lost soul. On one such occasion Abigail opened her heart to George telling him that she had no friends she could turn to and was so grateful for his support. It was clear to the more mature, sensitive people who knew Abigail that she hid a sad, vulnerable disposition. Even deeper could be found a sweetness that had become lost in benighted darkness. It was common knowledge in the village that Abigail Flint had quite a reputation with the boys but George began to see another side of her that was vulnerable, even sweet. He believed it was his duty to be the confidante that Abi needed.

As they sat drinking tea together on the sofa one day Abi began to get tearful and George put his arm around her in a comforting, fatherly way. It seemed to Abi that she felt she owed him more; it was the way her mind worked and this had become a pattern in her life. She was used to boys taking advantage of her and believed it was the way men wanted her to show her gratitude to them. They sat together, with George's arm around her, for a few moments. Then Abi turned her face to George and kissed his cheek. George didn't react immediately and she touched his face pulling it down onto her waiting lips. George didn't or couldn't pull away. As their lips touched gently he experienced something he'd never felt before; his heart was pounding in his chest; he was losing control.

Afterwards, George felt such guilt. He felt he'd taken advantage of Abi's vulnerability and was almost in tears with remorse.

'George, we are meant to be. I love you, truly.' Abi stroked his cheek tenderly.

'You don't know what you're saying Abi, you're upset. I must go.' George couldn't look at the girl.

'No George, please don't go, please.' She held on to his open shirt refusing to let him go; again he relented.

His emotions controlled his every thought and deed. No matter how hard he fought his alter ego, it always won. George was lost in an unfamiliar world and he didn't know how to put things right. The truth was simple, he couldn't put it right. He could never undo the betrayal and to continue the deceit was so painful for George. He had to think! He'd betrayed his wife and his faith and he didn't know how to stop it. So he didn't! His visits continued as did his adultery with this young girl. His life became unreal with emotions that were new and wonderful and frightening.

His diary became coded so that Daphne wouldn't become suspicious as the visits to Abigail increased. They would sometimes go for a ride in the car and, weather permitting, they sometimes ate a picnic that Abi would prepare for them. A simple thing like taking a walk in a nearby wood was exciting to George; they'd leave the car somewhere out of sight to passersby and walk hand in hand like young and free lovers. Of course they weren't, and George was in constant turmoil, but those times with his Abi were becoming too precious to give up. He was trapped in a web of deceit and lies and desire that he'd never known before.

As a young couple he and Daphne had decided to wait for marriage before consummating their relationship. It was a joint decision that seemed appropriate for a man of the cloth. They had known each other as friends for so long there didn't seem any hurry and considered themselves in control concerning matters of the flesh. Even on their wedding night there was very little excitement; neither had previous relationships and accepted the situation as being normal.

With Abigail Flint things were so very different. He was in love in a way he never believed possible and soon realised he had to be true to himself and Daphne; his wife had to be told.

It was such an enormous decision for George; he would lose his wife for sure and maybe his daughter. She would never forgive him. He knew that what he had done was beyond forgiveness and was sure that Daphne would never want to see him again. He deluded himself into believing there may be a slim chance she would allow contact with Louise but deep in his soul he knew he couldn't have it all. Then there was the ministry, he would have to leave the parish in shame and try to get some sort of work to support himself and Abi; but what? The only thing he had ever done was Theology; he had betrayed every one, including God.

Chapter 7

June 2011 - The Confession

Daphne had been concerned for some time about George and the demand his work commitments had on his time. In her opinion he worked far too hard and the hours out of the house were growing. George had never been a big man but recently had lost weight and began to look thin and drawn. His clothes were beginning to hang on his frame, his cheeks were hollow and he looked pale. He had been skipping meals at home and even when Daphne gave him a sandwich to eat whilst he was out he would bring it home uneaten. Daphne put it down to overwork and exhaustion but had given some thought to the realisation that there may be an underlying health problem that George was keeping from her. It seemed that they never had time to talk any more and no opportunity to bring her concerns casually into the conversation. They used to spend the odd afternoon together but it seemed he was always with one parishioner or another. Daphne always loved those afternoons when Louise was at school and she and George would have a cup of tea in the parlour looking out onto the garden. Without exception George would end up falling asleep in his comfy arm chair but Daphne was content to just be with him and often covered him as he slept with one of her crocheted blankets.

Little did the innocent Daphne know what was to come and how her world would be turned upside down. George and Abigail Flint had come to a decision that telling their respective families was for the best and for the good of all concerned. They both believed that they should admit to their adultery and leave the village together. It was the correct thing to do and they believed it should come out sooner than later. They had no concept of the havoc it would cause and the pain that would be suffered by those left behind to pick up the pieces in the wake of the lovers' exodus from Camberley Edge. It is said that confession is good for the soul, but certainly not in this case.

On that dreadful day, the Reverend George Anderson had been out since early morning coming home around 3 p.m. He had been with Abigail discussing their plans and attempting to get the timings right for a smooth exit. As George walked in through the front door of the vicarage, Daphne went to the hallway to greet him as usual, with an unaffectionate peck on his cheek.

'You look tired love. I'll put the kettle on and we'll have a nice cup of tea. Would you like a slice of sponge, dear? Freshly made and still a little warm.' Daphne started to walk towards the kitchen but stopped in her tracks when she heard the words that followed her.

'I don't want anything to eat or drink Daphne; I want to speak to you. Now!'

'Oh, that sounds ominous,' Daphne laughed as she joined him in the front parlour where he was sitting waiting for her.

George had taken his position in his usual chair, the large green leather winged armchair next to the fireplace. He looked even paler than usual to Daphne, who had stopped smiling and had a look of concern on her face. Whatever George had on his mind it was serious, so Daphne obediently took her place in the remaining armchair opposite her husband and waited. Her heartbeat got faster as she believed that George had bad news regarding his health; she was terrified but never expected what was to come.

The confession began, during which George never admitted to Daphne just how long the affair had been going on or even how it began. His tears told her one thing but his words were cold and emotionless, even robotic and rehearsed. He took pride in the fact that he was giving her the news and it was not coming from a gossip in the village. His words told her that he and Abigail had both fought against the attraction they had for each other and had prayed to God to show them the way forward. The story went on with a revelation of reasons and excuses starting with his obligation to console the poor Abigail her during her mother's illness. How he had felt it his duty and also necessary to be with her again after the premature death of her dear mother. George claimed that it was his Christian duty to be of support during the mourning period.

Daphne sat in wide eyed silence not understanding the words coming from her husband lips. Trying to speak, the only response she managed were 'George' and 'why?' Her heart was beating so fast it made her feel dizzy and she felt her cheeks begin to burn. His words were distant and faint as if she were a spectator to this nightmare and it couldn't possibly be true or real.

Daphne was beginning to understand what the changes in George over the past months meant, the changes in his pattern of work and the hours he was out visiting with his so-called parishioners. Everything was falling into place. Her body sunk deeper into the armchair as the reality of what George was saying took her strength away. He had been with Abigail Flint when her father Edward was out at work. Daphne's mind was racing as she imagined them together and tears began to fall down her cheeks. George didn't need to paint a picture of what adultery was and he consciously left out most of the details, but Daphne knew. He also omitted to say that Abigail gave him excitement with an overbearing presence of lustful motivation which was lacking in their marriage.

George expected to feel something good after telling Daphne what he thought was a heart felt confession; but that didn't happen. The words poured out, in an almost childlike version of truth. George never said he wasn't to blame yet gave reasons for his adultery as if he wasn't responsible for the pain and heartache he was causing his devoted wife.

'Villagers have never understood her delicate nature, Daphne,' he tried to argue the point that Abigail wasn't as bad as the gossip suggested. 'I have come to know her and she's a good person. She is devastated over what we've done to you; really she is.'

'You could have stopped George; you could have tried harder.' She sobbed the words.

Daphne knew, as did the whole village that Abigail had no friends to turn to. The girls she had gone to school with didn't have Abigail's sex appeal and were jealous of her. She always had dates with handsome young men. She knew what they wanted and it wasn't her friendship, but she inevitably conceded to their requests or demands. In George, she had found an honest person who was willing to do the right thing by her; but not, sadly, by his wife.

The only job Abigail Flint had since leaving school was in the village pub, The Swan, and she was perfect for the job. When Mrs Flint was diagnosed with cancer Abigail was able to spend time during the day with her sick mother and her Dad took over the care in the evenings so that she could go to work when the pub opened. Working and flirting, in the pub at night took Abigail's mind off her troubles. She'd laugh and joke with all the customers until the end of her shift and by the time she got home, her parents would be fast asleep in bed, which was often a relief to her.

Was this the girl that was stealing Daphne's husband? It was inconceivable that he could be so ridiculously gullible and allow this to happen to their marriage. He continued with his absurd reasons for the whole disgusting affair. Daphne had a feeling of mixed emotions; anger mainly. George tried to explain to Daphne that it was always his intention to just show kindness to Abigail when her mother finally passed. He left out the bit where his kindness was reciprocated by an offer he couldn't refuse. Of course he should have refused and it was later verbalised by the villagers who morally condemned him; they made it clear that his behaviour was wholly inappropriate and higher standards were expected of a man of the cloth. No one could argue with that, not even George.

The confession was not too detailed. He purposely avoided words that would create an image of the times he spent in the arms of his young lover even though Daphne asked. George made a conscious effort to omit the picnics in the country which always ended with Abigail showing an alfresco version of her usual appreciation. He tried not to hurt her more than he already had; so when George felt the confession was complete he told Daphne that a decision had already been made and there was no room for discussion on the matter. Of that George was extremely clear.

George got up and went to Daphne pulling her up towards him. They cried in each others arms.

'I'll always love you Daph, but I can't go on like this anymore.'

'What have I done to make you do this to us, George?'

'You've done nothing, my love; I've been the weak one.'

'Please don't leave us George. I'll be a better wife to you and we'll put this mess behind us and start afresh.'

George didn't reply. It was the end and it broke Daphne's heart. They just stood together in each other's arms and wept.

That day would remain in Louise's memory for the rest of her life. It was about a month before the village Flower Festival and Daphne had been working so hard to get things done, spending very little time at home apart from caring for her delightful array of orchids which lived not only in her elaborate green house but in various suitable locations all over the house. It was a familiar pattern running up to the Flower Festival with Daphne planning and organising the whole thing, mostly on her own but doing a perfect job.

Louise realised afterwards that the confession had probably started sometime during the afternoon in the parlour which was the place serious talking went on. The parlour as far as she was aware was normally reserved for visitors so Louise knew, on her arrival home from school that day, that something serious was afoot.

Daphne had shouted as she heard Louise come in through the front door.

'Darling! Go and make yourself a sandwich in the kitchen sweetheart. I'll be out soon.'

Her voice sounded strange but Louise didn't really take much notice until she heard her mother crying. Going straight into the parlour she saw her father with his arms around her mum and they were both crying. He never gave Louise an explanation; he left that to Daphne.

His words were short but not sweet.

'Louise, my princess. I love you so much. Daddy has to go away so I want you to be brave for me and mum.'

'Tell her the truth George; she's old enough to understand.'

George couldn't speak so Daphne spat out the hateful words with anger and damaged pride.

'Daddy's got a girlfriend and they are going away together. He doesn't love us anymore.'

'Oh Daphne! Please don't,' George pleaded.

'I hate you.' Screamed Louise. 'I hate you and I'll hate you forever.' The young girl ran to her mother's arms and cried pitifully.

There was no more to be said. George went upstairs and came down almost immediately with a packed suitcase that he'd hidden under the bed. He left never to be seen again.

On reflection there must have been quite a lot of arranging before the great confession, a vicar just can't up and leave but that was exactly what it looked like. They heard later that there had been a scuffle at the tart's house. Abigail's father was extremely angry and wanted to flatten George when he arrived to collect her. Mr Flint didn't really know his daughter and believed the affair to be totally George Anderson's fault. What had been planned as a dignified exit turned into a circus with Edward Flint pushing and shoving George in the street and Abigail trying to intervene.

'Dad please! It's not George's fault we couldn't help ourselves.' Things were getting out of control and Edward Flint, being the larger of the two men, was gaining control, or some would say, losing it completely.

'You disgusting animal George Anderson, I trusted you. I trusted my daughter in your care as a vicar and father. What about your wife, George? What does she think about all this? Hey?'

With one movement George was flung across the bonnet of his get-away car and Edward was on top of him. The street was filling up with spectators who had heard the commotion. Madge and Bob were running up the street from their post office. Someone had run to get them knowing they were close friends of the vicar and with the belief that they could help the situation.

Bob shouted as he ran. 'Ed, stop it. What d'you think you are doing?'

'Mind your own business, Bob;' shouted Edward Flint, 'this good-for-nothing, so-called vicar is trying to run off with my daughter. Now what do you think of your friend? I'm going to kill him.'

Bob matched Edward Flint's stature and was able to wrestle him to the ground before he could do serious damage to George; although there were already a few scratches on George's face. Once free from Ed's grip George grabbed Abigail and her bag and they got in the car. Within a second all you could see was the red estate car speeding up the street to the sound and smell of the rubber tyres burning on the tarmac.

Somehow the adulterers made their escape leaving everyone flabbergasted. Most of the village, Madge and Bob alongside Edward Flint, just stood in the middle of the road in shock and amazement.

Madge suddenly thought of her friend Daphne and without a word ran to the vicarage to consol her and Louise. What could possibly have happened to cause all this? Madge thought as she ran through the vicarage gate and in through the open front door. Her heart broke when she saw the two huddled together on the floor in the parlour, trying to console one and other. The two were clinging together as they sobbed in each others arms. Madge had no words so she fell to the floor with her beloved friend and held them both until the sobbing ebbed.

For once the sleepy little village of Camberley Edge finally had some real gossip and they made the most of it. The story escalated as each detail was repeated from one neighbour to another in Chinese whispers. Most witnessed the great exodus of George Anderson and Abigail Flint but the reasons behind it all were fair game to the gossips. Most of them professing to have inside knowledge of the events but no-one really knowing or giving a second thought to the pain that it was all causing Daphne and Louise.

Little did the gossips know that there was much more to come as the saga of the Andersons continued and what was to follow was unheard of in the lifetime of Camberley Edge.

Chapter 8

Life without George

It was a hard time for Daphne and Louise; the embarrassment mostly. They closed ranks and discouraged visitors who wanted to come to sympathise, or, in most cases, find out the sordid details. The discouragement didn't work for very long and they went through many cups of tea and packets of biscuits. Those that were 'in the know' gave them the unwanted advice that they shouldn't spend time worrying about a man who could leave his family for such an adulterous tart. Of course, words like that rarely help; they only served to devalue the good times that George and Daphne had shared. Slowly the visitors and the unwanted advice stopped and they began to get on with their lives. Louise concentrated on her school work with vigour and determination; what else was there to do?

For the first time ever, Daphne hadn't given a second thought to the village flower festival, and it came and went without her.

Daphne had been granted a short period of time in the vicarage but it was ultimately needed for the new vicar and his family. It wasn't long before they found a small cottage on the outskirts of the village, which they could rent until their financial position was evaluated. They moved in as soon as they could. Moving wasn't too difficult as most of the furniture in the vicarage came with the house and had to remain there. But that also meant that Daphne had to buy new.

Friends and neighbours realised their predicament and supported Daphne by offering items of furniture for their new home to help until their financial situation improved.

Louise's possessions, that she had outgrown, were left at the vicarage in the hope that the next vicar would have a daughter who could enjoy the garden house and the princess bedroom that Louise had loved so much.

It was discussed at length and finally decided that the many books George had accumulated over the years would be put into storage.

The owner of the new property lived in the village and Daphne knew him well. The house had been up for sale for a long time but under the circumstances he was happy to let Daphne rent it for a while. It had three small bedrooms and bathroom upstairs. Downstairs the rooms were again small and fairly typical of a cottage that hadn't been changed over the years. A sitting room, dining room and a fairly modern kitchen with room for a small table and chairs. The vicarage it wasn't, but it was cosy and Daphne felt it was a good start. It was such a relief to be out of the home they'd shared with George and the sad memories of the last couple of months.

Christmas came and went and the only contact from George was a card for Louise and a cheque for £50. It was delivered to Madge at the village post office, George obviously didn't know where they had moved to and he knew Madge would pass it on to Louise. Receiving the card brought back the sad memories of the past few months and broke his little girl's heart. The cheque was never cashed.

As spring arrived and the weather improved, Daphne started work on the garden. It hadn't had any attention for many years, so getting it into shape wasn't easy. The plan was that there would be a small plot for vegetables and salad stuff, a border for herb and flower beds strategically placed for effect. The picture in Daphne's mind soon transferred to her back garden after a lot of hard graft and imagination. Her one pride and joy was her small pond and water feature, it was made entirely out of rocks and stones that had been dug out of the soil. Once the base had been put in place by the man from the local garden centre along with the electrics for the pump, for a price of course, the black liner was laid and the small pond was filled with water. Daphne arranged the rocks and stones around the top and bought stone creatures which were randomly placed around the edges. The electric pump and filter ensured clear bubbling water at all times which was a pleasure to sit near on a warm evening. Maybe even a few small coy carp would be homed there in the future. Who knows?

There had to be greenhouses eventually but for the time being just one was erected for her on the corner, at the end of the vegetable plot and in the sun all day; ideal for Daphne's seedlings to be nurtured. Again she called in an expert to install heating ready for the winter but all the other jobs she did alone and often took a cup of tea into the garden and sat with a huge, smug smile on her face admiring her kingdom.

At last the pain was easing and her life was reforming without George. There was more smiling and even laughter. Life was become more bearable and improving each day. Both Daphne and Louise engaged in every activity in the village they could, which kept them busy. It took their minds off 'the evil one,' although they did seem to find time to discuss his despicable behaviour most evenings. No matter how hard they tried, the after dinner conversation always turns to George.

The village was renowned for the Flower Festival that took place every July. People would travel for miles to compete in the various flower arranging competitions and there was always a great selection of beautiful plants on display and for sale. Amongst others, the orchid growers would bring a beautiful selection of their best and rarest in the hope of a first prize which would feed their ego but also hold them in good stead in their field of expertise. Competition was rife, something Daphne encouraged. The usual over-sized vegetables would be displayed and, in some ways, the growers of the gigantic marrows and slightly rude carrots were even more competitive than the orchid fanciers. Others visitors would simply come for the day out, to enjoy a strawberry tea and take in the wonderful creations. Daphne had been the committee chairman for years and also exhibited her own flowers and beautiful orchids. Along with flowers, plants and vegetables there were stalls of every kind, from home produce to baking and handy-crafts. The Camberley Edge Annual Flower Festival really was quite something and raised not only a good sum of cash each year but also the profile of an otherwise unknown village.

With her new job at Madge's post office, which was also the general store and cafe, Daphne was always busy but never too busy to read about and discover new and exciting species of orchid. She had belonged to the British Orchid Growers Association for a few years and often showed her orchids at other flower festivals and orchid shows all over the country, making new friends at each event.

It had been George who encouraged her to go on an organised trip to Ecuador with The Orchid Society of Great Britain. She argued that he and Louise wouldn't manage without her, but they did, and she had a wonderful time.

It had been her dream come true to see the Dracula Vampira (Luer) in its natural habitat on the slopes of Mount Pichincha in Ecuador. It is such a fragile orchid and extremely rare, yet it grows on mossy trees attached by its roots and quenched by the moss which keeps it alive and healthy. The orchid thrives at 1,800 to 2,200 metres above sea level in cool cloud drenched forests. Although the sepals are green the flower has a much darker hue due to the purple black veins that converge at the tip. This orchid can also be seen at Kew where its habitat is duplicated by mounting it onto cork oak bark with moss, keeping the roots moist.

Anything related to orchids and Daphne was first in line. At night she would read the latest orchid magazines to find out as much as she could about the latest discoveries all over the world. Going to Kew Gardens was rarely an option for her; the best experience had to be in the wild, seeing them where they had grown without any help from mankind.

Apart from a few extra-curricular activities, Louise's life was mostly about school; she was not entirely certain of what she wanted to eventually do as regards a career and had decided to take a varied selection of G.C.S.E. exam subjects in order to keep her options open. A keen reader, Louise loved her books and spent hours at the local library. She had little interest in technology and found the modern day reading gadgets cold and detached; there was nothing like the feel of a well-loved book as far as Louise was concerned. She had so many traits which remind Daphne that her only daughter was not only the living image of George but like him in so many other ways too.

Louise had inherited her father's clear, lateral thinking process which had taken him and his faith into Theology and the sharing of the Word of God with others. With the same abilities it would take Louise in a different direction which both her parents had thought might be Law. George had realised that, from an early age, Louise had the ability to stand her ground in an argument. Bedtime was always interesting when she would protest that television programmes could, in fact, be educational and her parents should be more open to reason and allow her some say in the matter. Of course soap operas couldn't be classed as such but the debate was always good, inevitably leading to Louise taking a bath and an early night. Louise could always give a good account of herself which pleased her dad, making him proud of his little girl. Sadly, with George leaving home, things wouldn't go quite as planned for Louise and university became a far off dream.

Daphne often thought about George; how he was and what he was doing, often wondering if he was still with 'the tart' and if they were happy together but hoping they weren't. Even if they weren't it was too late for him and Daphne now. After all the pain and deception there was no way back even if George had wanted one. Well, at least that's what she told everyone else. It seemed that it was what her friends expected to hear. In reality, time had softened Daphne's anger towards George and she began to contemplate the life they had lived together as man and wife; how things could have been if she had worked harder at their marriage instead of giving up so easily as George had done. If only she had known what was to come then maybe she could have prevented it, and she would still have her George. In times of reflection it was easier for Daphne to blame Abigail Flint for her pain rather than George. That woman had taken advantage of his kind nature and weaknesses to steal him away from his family; but those thoughts and beliefs never lessened the pain.

Some nights were more difficult than others, wondering what she had done wrong or how she could have been a better wife to George; then perhaps he wouldn't have turned to another woman for love. That was the worse thing for Daphne, imagining her George making love to another woman. She had always known that she was not the best as far as bedroom antics were concerned but she was a virgin when she married George and she genuinely believed he loved her for it.

Busy days and lonely nights; was this to be her future?

Chapter 9

Early June 2013 - The Arrival of Alex

It was the second anniversary of Georges' departure. No-one had seen or heard from him apart from birthday and Christmas cards for Louise with the usual cheque for £50 which was never cashed. He had disappeared completely and no-one even cared; well, except for Daphne. As far as everyone was concerned she was over the love rat but there were times when she almost felt forgiveness for the way he had treated her; on occasions even blaming herself. After two years it seemed that she would never see George again but that didn't stop her wondering what was happening in his life.

Sadly, apart from the flower festival there had been very little going on in the lives of Daphne and Louise since he left, at least, nothing until a few weeks before the festival was due to begin when a new couple set up home in the village. News travels fast in a small community like Camberley Edge and newcomers are rare so it was soon common knowledge that they were a young married couple who had come up from London and had taken up residence in old Mrs Crawshay's cottage. Edward Crawshay had been a retired military officer of some standing who had passed away over twenty years ago. There were no children to take care of his widow, Camilla, when she began to fail both physically and mentally and was now in her late eighties. Although the neighbours were good to Camilla by doing her shopping and some light housework, it was inevitable that she would end up having to go into a care home with nursing facilities and it followed that the house had to be sold to pay the costs.

Although it was called a cottage, it was bigger than most of the houses in Camberley Edge. It had an enormous rambling garden that Edward used to plant with every vegetable you could think of when he was fit and well and there were several fruit trees that Mrs Crawshay called 'the orchard'.

Camilla was quite a snob in her day but had a heart of gold and always helped to finance the activities of the village right up until the end. When Edward Crawshay passed away, she became more proactive and put herself forward for an active position on the Village Flower Festival Committee. Her generous donations probably secured her place on the committee and she revelled in her new life. Sadly, in time, she became unable to continue with her committee work and was, for the most part, housebound but she had many visitors who helped her get along for a while. Camilla was missed by all who knew her when she was eventually taken into a nursing home in a town several miles away.

The cottage that Edward and Camilla shared for many years had a sweet name that Camilla Crawshay had chosen when they first moved in as a young married couple. Jasmine Cottage. There was no Jasmine around their front door for a few years but Camilla knew her mind and eventually the name suited the cottage. After many years of steady growth and nurturing it not only grew around the door but has spread throughout the front garden which you could smell as you passed by. In full bloom, the Jasmine has such a powerful scent passers by would stop for a moment and enjoy the sweetness of its fragrance.

The cottage was thought to be a good buy for a young couple prepared to carry out the repairs and update it; with a little love and attention it would make a good family home. No-one understood why Camilla called the house Jasmine Cottage. They could accept the Jasmine part but it certainly wasn't a typical cottage. It did have smallish front windows but the rest of its features were far from small. The rooms were large and the ceilings high and the entrance hall had a magnificent staircase, open on both sides with a huge landing at the top which led to three large bedrooms and a bathroom. Camilla was well-bred and well-educated; she had married Edward, who was a serving officer in the army, and happened to be a good friend of one of her brothers. Her father was also a military man and she had two brothers who followed suit. Her home reflected this with family photos on every sideboard and on the beautiful grand piano which dominated the lounge, and which Camilla played exquisitely.

Daphne and Louise were having a late tea in the garden one warm July evening, enjoying the sunset and chatting about the imminent arrival of the flower festival that Daphne loved so much. Her enthusiasm always seemed to filter down to Louise who tried to help in small ways.

'Darling! Why don't you go around to Jasmine Cottage and introduce yourself to the new couple. You could take them a couple of entry tickets for the flower festival. A sort of welcome gesture from the festival committee, a show of kindness. They would be able to get to know the villagers and break the ice a little. I'm sure having chosen to live here they would want to be part of our way of life, so being at the festival would give them the opportunity to speak with every one and maybe make friends.' Daphne laughed 'Everyone who's anyone will be there, as usual.'

Louise wasn't really keen but agreed to go anyway. Daphne went to get a pair of tickets and said to her daughter as she handed them to her.

'No time like the present sweetheart.'

Jasmine Cottage was just a couple of streets behind the High Street backing onto open fields; she took the tickets and went to deliver them. Louise had never been good with strangers. She lacked confidence with those she didn't know and since she had reached puberty there were a few surplus pounds gathering around her hips which made her feel even worse. Louise thought of herself as goofy and relied on her personality to make a good impression, but the truth was that her red hair and pale complexion became more appealing as she grew older and her childhood 'rabbit-like' teeth looked less pronounced as her face grew to fit them. She began to stand out from the crowd but in a good way now.

As she walked into the front garden the sweet smell of the jasmine welcomed her but she wondered if the newcomers would mind her intrusion. She tapped hesitantly on the front door and it opened almost immediately. He stood there, like an

Adonis with short black curly hair and very broad shoulders. He had on shorts and a tight fitting T-shirt, slightly soiled, as if he'd been working in the garden. Louise couldn't help looking at his thighs which had muscles that she didn't know existed. In fact his whole body was honed to perfection; he must spend hours in the gym, thought Louise, unable to form a word. Fortunately she didn't have to speak but she did have to force her eyes up to his face as he spoke.

'I saw you coming down the path,' was the explanation of his eagerness in opening the front door.

'Please come in.' He gestured her into the large lounge.

'All the rooms are still full of boxes I'm afraid. Please sit down if you can find a space.' His pleasant disposition and laugh were contagious. Louise giggled in her child-like way, looking around for an uncluttered space to sit.

Sitting herself down in the nearest empty chair, she explained her visit holding out the tickets for him to take. He rubbed his hands together in a gesture of removing any dirt and took the tickets, placing them on the bare mantle piece.

'That's so kind of you to think of us, we'd be delighted to come.'

Louise hadn't been in Mrs Crawshay's home for a long time. The last time was probably with her mother when she was a small child but it looked exactly as she remembered it. The carpets were the same but very worn, almost threadbare, and there were quite a few pieces of Mrs Crawshay's old, antique furniture still there. It smelled a bit like an 'old person's home' as her mother would say. It indeed needed some work and a lot of fresh air.

Her host could see her looking around the room and interjected.

'Have you been in the house before?'

'Only as a small child, I think, with my mother.'

'We plan on doing some work on the inside in time, you know, painting and new carpets. For now, I have to build kennels and workshops in the back garden so that I can make a living. I want to breed working dogs.'

54

'That sounds exciting, I love animals.' Louise smiled sweetly in awe of this man.

They chatted for a while, about half an hour. Louise was comfortably relaxed in his company and told him all about the flower festival and what to expect. Her enthusiasm showed as she explained every detail of the event.

'My mother grows the most amazing orchids. People come from all over just to see them and she sells them too.'

'And what do you do?' he asked, changing the subject to slow the excited girl down a little.

Taking a nervous breath she replied 'Oh! Nothing really, I'm just in school, you know starting my 'A' levels in September. I'm planning on studying Law and Accountancy. I have a job lined up in an accountancy firm where my mother used to work'.

'Not going to university then? You could go forward with Law.'

'Oh no, I'm content with staying here in Camberley Edge.'

Louise was going to explain that leaving her mother wasn't an option for her at the moment but decided against pouring her heart out to a complete stranger. There were a few seconds silence.

Louise sat there wondering where his wife was, there was no other sounds in the house.

As if reading her mind he said.

'My wife works in London and commutes daily. She should be home soon. It's a shame you've missed her.'

As much as she tried not to, she found herself asking about his wife.

'What does your wife do in London?'

'She's a solicitor for the defence, and works in adult criminal courts and also youth courts where she defends youngsters up to the age of eighteen years. The only problem with criminal law is that you have to be on call day and night. When a client breaks the law and gets arrested, they rarely offend during working hours. They don't work nine to five.' The handsome Adonis had the most amazing laugh.

Louise was enjoying herself, but suddenly realised that she had been there for while and her mother would be wondering why she was so long. Getting up suddenly she smiled and bowed her head in her modest way as she walked toward the front door explaining that her mother would get worried. The handsome young man got up and moved quickly to the door ahead of Louise, opening it for her. She looked up into his eyes. He was tall. Tall and strong and handsome and everything wonderful.

'Thank you,' the corners of her mouth quivered slightly as she smiled. She ran down the path and through the front gate into the street.

'Thanks for the tickets,' he shouted after her. 'They are a lovely thought.'

Louise waved in acknowledgement as she walked away from the house. Her long legs carried her home on a cushion of air. She felt exhilarated and happier than she had ever been. Her heart was beating so fast she thought she would faint with excitement and she just couldn't get that picture of him in the shorts and T-shirt out of her head. And those thighs! They were something else. He was so nice as well, she thought, as she floated into the television room where her mother was sitting. Yes, she thought, so very, very, very nice.

'Hi Lou! Were they in?'

'Yes mum. They were glad that we had thought of them and they'll be at the festival.' Louise really wasn't in the mood for a chat and was pleased when her mother continued to concentrate on the film she had been watching on the television.

That night Louise found it difficult to get off to sleep, thoughts of her meeting with that handsome young man were bouncing around in her head when she suddenly sat bolt upright in bed.

'I forgot to ask his name! Oh Louise you are such an idiot,' she scolded herself.

Sleep led her into a world of dreams, some of which her mother would not have been proud, and certainly not familiar to the innocent Louise.

Morning came and for once Louise didn't have to be called; she was up, dressed and eager for the day ahead. That afternoon she walked home alone from school and decided to pass by his house, a little out of her way but she couldn't help herself. He was nowhere to be seen but she could hear his dogs in the back garden. Tempted as she was to go around the back, she walked past and straight home.

'Louise? Is that you?'

'Of course Mum, who were you expecting?'

'Alex' Daphne said as she walked into the lounge from the kitchen.

'Who is Alex?' Louise questioned without concern.

'Well, you should know you were in his house last night.' A huge smile spread across Louise's face as she thought 'What a perfect name for a perfect guy.'

Just at that moment in walked Alex.

'Oh! Alex' said Daphne 'I haven't had time to speak to her yet. She's just come home from school.'

'Louise,' he looked at her with those big brown eyes. 'Would you mind helping me out this weekend?'

Louise was bursting and almost said yes before he told her what he wanted.

'Susannah and I are going to London this weekend to the wedding of some close friends. I was going to take the dogs to Wales for my parents to look after them but I thought you might like to do it and, of course, I'll pay you for your time.'

It all fell into place now. Louise knew they had come up from London to live in Camberley Edge but there was something in Alex's accent that she couldn't quite place. He was eloquently spoken and his diction was perfect which she attributed to his Welsh upbringing.

'You don't have to pay me Alex. I'd be happy to help out. How many dogs do you have?'

'Just the four at the moment, two Labradors, and two Spaniels. You only have to let them out in the morning and evening, they'll run in the fields behind the cottage and always come back when you call, they're good dogs. Oh, and feed them of course before you let them out in the evening and make sure their water bowls are full.'

'I'd love to look after the dogs Alex, but I think I should get to know them first.'

'That's a good idea, Lou,' Daphne agreed and laughed as she said, 'You'll have a job to get rid of her now she knows you have dogs. She always wanted one as a child but we never got around to getting one.'

'That suits me fine Mrs Anderson. When my business is up and running I'll need lots of help, paid even.' Alex teased.

'Daphne, please call me Daphne. It's good to meet you, Alex, and I hope you'll be happy in Camberley Edge; it's a great place to live.'

Alex left the Anderson's home with a smile on his face and knew that they had made the right decision to move there. It was his dream come true. Little did he know what was in store.

Louise called into Jasmine Cottage every night from school that week, before Susannah got home. She considered it an adventure and she loved the dogs never having had one of her own.

Louise would talk with Alex about his plans for dogs breeding. He adored his dogs and wanted to build a reputation for training them and their puppies to a high standard for working.

Alex was already talking to local farmers and landowners about organising events on their land. He had found a few who were interested in an organised shoot. Alex had ideas that would not only be lucrative but would draw people to the village from all around. He would provide the dogs from his stock and men from the village who wanted to help and earn a little cash at the same time.

He explained to Louise.

'There are many types of birds that can be shot and eaten like pheasant and partridge.' Alex had a child-like charm when they spoke together of his plans and Louise was becoming dangerously besotted with her Adonis.

Alex had started construction on the outbuildings he needed to breed and train these dogs in. It would be hard work and take some time but his enthusiasm and energy was not lacking. His wife, Susannah seemed to work very hard at her job in the city; well she spent a lot of time there. Alex was sometimes alone several evenings each week when Susannah was on call and had to stay at their London apartment, to be near if needed. Louise was delighted to keep him company.

On one of her visits Alex was in the back garden and Louise went to look for him.

'Hi Alex, I hope you don't mind me coming around the back. You couldn't hear me knocking the front door.'

'No, of course not, I'm grateful. You can see all my hard work.' He laughed.

'Gosh Alex! The buildings are bigger than I imagined. It must have been hard for you to do this all on your own.'

'No, I've had a lot of help from local builders. I had help to draw up the plans for the buildings; I knew what I wanted them to look like but there is so much more to know. You need a water supply and electricity and I had to take down the side wall to allow access onto the property for large machinery and somewhere to keep my vehicles. It's really never ending and has caused me some sleepless nights, but I think it will pay off in the end.' Alex gave her one of his special smiles; she noticed how lovely his teeth were.

Alex continued.

'Most of the construction work was done before we moved in. I travelled up to check on things at the weekends. My wife thought it would be less intrusive to have the builders off the premises before we took up residence. It worked out for the best. So I hope to do the rest of the work myself and save some money.'

Louise was mesmerised. Not only was he extremely handsome, he was clever too.

Chapter 10

Late July 2013 - The Day of the Flower Festival.

The annual village flower festival was yet again another success. Daphne's orchids won her first place in the orchid grower's competition, as usual; she also won a few other competitions but to win with her orchids was always her aim and she seemed to be getting better each year with no other grower coming even close. The local press were out in force to take photographs of the very prestigious judges from all over the country. It always made good reading and raised the profile of an otherwise sleepy and unknown village. The press photographer had taken a photo of Daphne with the prize winning orchids and she hoped that would be printed too. She also loved the attention she got from other orchid growers who were keen to find out her trade secrets and for the most part she'd give them the advice they wanted even offering her time and a possible visit to her home and amazing greenhouses to see some of the rare types she was nurturing.

Alex and his wife Susannah came along for the afternoon; it was the first time for Louise to meet her, in fact the first time for any of the villagers to meet her. Louise walked towards the couple when she saw them looking at the Women's Institute stall with their delicious and expertly decorated home made cakes and, of course the famous home made jam.

'Hi Alex, this must be Susannah,' said Louise with a friendly smile.

Susannah turned to see who was so familiar with her husband. Louise had expected her to be nice looking but Susannah was amazingly beautiful. Her makeup was perfect; with dark eyeliner and distinctive eyebrows framing her small but perfect face. She wore a pale pink lipstick with gloss coating making her lips more voluptuous. Even to a young country girl like Louise, who wore very little makeup at all, she knew what it took to look that good. Susannah's clothes were simple; a pair of blue jeans a white T shirt and no jewellery apart from her wedding ring. Understated glamour, Louise thought, but with a figure like that she needed nothing more.

Louise was in awe of this beauty before her. Even the way she stood gave off an air of confidence. It was difficult for the young girl to draw her eyes away from the elegant Susannah.

Alex spoke and Louise smiled eagerly.

'Darling, this is Louise. She gave us the tickets.'

'Oh yes, I'm pleased to meet you Louise and thank you for the tickets.'

'You're welcome.' Louise was a little put out by Susannah's formality.

'I must thank you for looking after Alex's dogs for us to go to the wedding the other weekend. Very kind of you. I hope he paid you well.' Susannah smiled condescendingly.

'Now, darling this is quite enough country life for one day. I'll just buy a small jar of jam and we'll be off.' Turning to Louise she said with a smile, 'Thank you once again Louise, goodbye dear.'

Alex smiled at Louise and thanked her once more for the tickets as Susannah paid for the jam. The couple left.

Louise watched them walk away and felt relieved that she hadn't warmed to Susannah. It made liking Alex easier and would ease her conscience when she fell asleep at night with him on her mind. Daphne suddenly ran past Louise and chased after Alex as they headed for the exit.

They were near the exit when Daphne caught up with them, a little breathless. She had a pot plant in her hand offering it to them. Susannah looked at the plant for a while before taking it.

'Oh, my word. Does this need a lot of care? I'm afraid I have little confidence in this surviving with my lack of experience of plants.' Susannah laughed but it really wasn't very funny and Daphne's face told that she wasn't well pleased and continued to speak, ignoring the comment.

'It's a Miltoniopsis 'Red Tide' but is commonly known as the Pansy Orchid.' Looking directly at Susannah she continued, 'I think you'll be able to keep it alive quite easily. It needs very little care. It's quite a sturdy little plant. Just keep it out of direct sunlight. A small gift from Louise and myself. It's one of my prettier orchids.'

Alex felt the tension and broke in.

'I was going to ask you Daphne; maybe next year at the festival I can show how my working dogs perform. The lake is not far away and I can get them to retrieve on command and do a few entertaining tricks.'

'Well we can certainly put that to the committee Alex. What a wonderful idea. I've seen working dogs at summer shows before and it always seems to entertain the crowds, especially the youngsters.'

Alex continued. 'A town in mid Wales near my home has a show each year. The Royal Welsh Show in Builth Wells; the dog performances always seem to go down well.'

'Yes, I've been to that show a few times and I've seen the dogs. Isn't it an agricultural show, Alex?'

'Primarily yes, but there are hundreds of shopping tents, café tents and even some permanent buildings. There's a great big arena where the farmers show their cattle and where various other shows are put on. They have the Cossack's horse riders and formal pageantry to name just a few; a wonderful display of talent. The show lasts for four days and is always full to capacity every day.'

'Well, we can't compete with that, Alex, but you've got me interested in your dogs for the next festival. You must come to the next committee meeting as my guest and we can put it forward together.'

'I'll be there Daphne, let me know when. Thank you.'

The couple left and Daphne noticed that Susannah passed the orchid to Alex for him to carry. Daphne was a compassionate lady and decided not to judge Susannah harshly on just one meeting and went back to work in the section she was in charge of.

With the Pansy Orchid in hand Alex and Susannah walked the short distance back to Jasmine Cottage. Alex broke the silence.

'They're nice aren't they, love?'

'Who? What?' Susannah was dismissive.

'Daphne, of course, and Louise.'

'Oh! Yes, they're lovely and the plant. Put it on the hall stand Alex, Daphne said not to put it direct sunlight.'

'I'm surprised you remember Su. You weren't very friendly.'

'Well they're not really my type of people, are they? You know country.'

'Really! Susannah. Your parents live in the country and you were raised there, weren't you?' Alex was becoming a little annoyed by Susannah's snobbery. What he found exciting and challenging when they first met was now becoming irritating.

Susannah continued totally unaware of Alex's mood. 'Well darling. There's country and there's country. My understanding of country life is sitting on a comfy chair set on a well manicured lawn drinking champagne and eating canapés whilst the help makes a delicious dinner.'

'But that's not everyone's world Su. That's a privileged one.'

'Really? How sad for them. I suppose you are going to tell me again about how hard your parents have to work in that Clandod place.'

'It's not Clandod. It's Llandrindod Wells.' He retorted curtly and went out to tend his beautiful dogs in the back garden. When Susannah was like this he had to get away from her before he lost control and it would end up in a massive fight. Since their first and last fight ended in a cheap slanging match which Susannah stretched out for nearly a month Alex avoided such arguments like the plague.

Yet another lovely day spoiled by the charming Susannah, he thought, as he sat on the grass surrounded by his four best friends, his beloved dogs. Alex loved Susannah dearly but he felt she never considered his feelings. At first their love

64

was so intense it ran in all directions, out of control but wonderful. His passion for her was still strong but he wondered how she really felt about him. Alex often asked her if she really loved him and the answer was always 'How can you ask? I adore you, my love.' Susannah was clever with words and always had the right answer waiting.

Time passed quickly and Alex hurriedly fed and walked his precious dogs before putting them into their kennels in the large out building and turning off the light. He went back into the kitchen, now in darkness. Putting on the light he saw a sandwich cling-filmed to a tea plate. It told him that Su was having an early night and was admitting just a little remorse for her behaviour earlier. The sandwich was smoked salmon and cream cheese on granary which he ate quickly and went upstairs in anticipation. He also had a beaming smile on his face when he saw what was awaiting him.

Chapter 11

2013 - Daphne's Plans as a Single Lady.

Daphne had worked so hard to make the Festival a success. The preparation for the show went on for months before, but for Daphne and her orchids it was a lifetime's work. Within a few weeks of showing her latest orchid she had orders from all over the country, even from experts who had heard of her new rare black orchid and wanted to know more. To her delight she was getting invitations to specialist orchid growing groups and giving talks about her success. Orchid growers are a special breed of gardener, dedicated and adoring of their product. It's not like cultivating other flowers and plants; it's much more difficult to grow an orchid from seed. The rarer genus of orchid are mostly indigenous to hot, humid climates and are pollinated naturally by insects native to that country which makes it difficult to replicate. To grow orchids from seeds in Great Britain is far more complicated and conditions have to be created which duplicate the climate and growing conditions of the country of origin. The correct humidity is important and 'flasking' with germination gel gives the seed a chance of turning into a beautiful flower. Without insects to help, pollination has to be done manually. The results are rewarding when all this work is successful and a beautiful orchid is created that everyone wants to own.

Since cultivating and growing the world's rarest orchids it had always been Daphne's desire to visit Chiang Mai in Northern Thailand where some of the most desirable orchids grow, and pay a visit to the 'Tropical Botanic Garden Chiang Mai' one of the most famous places in the world for rare orchids. The climate there is extremely humid and hot which is ideal for their development.

Daphne has a group of orchid enthusiast friends from all over the U.K. eager to join her on a visit to Chiang Mai but she was the only one prepared to make all the arrangements and it was complicated. The trip would have to be January or February as the climate would be better for the physical tolerance of the fussy British traveller. The weather at that time of year would be hot but less humid. To visit in our summer time would be risky as there is normally quite a lot of rain in Thailand at that time of year and mobility would be restricted.

She had planned the journey to start at Heathrow Airport and arrive at Bangkok, then another flight from Bangkok to Chiang Mai. The airport at Chiang Mai is the fourth largest in the country and very busy. Daphne wasn't much of a traveller and the thought of such a large foreign airport frightened her but going with friends would make it easier. Computers were not familiar to Daphne but fortunately she had Louise to help her. They used Google to find hotels in the region of Chiang Mai airport. The five star hotels were quite expensive but to stay in less would mean they would have to compromise. In fact those lower star hotels were dreadful and not comfortable enough to satisfy Daphne's group. The Shangri-La-Hotel near the old city seemed perfect, especially when the on-line write up said the staff spoke perfect English and would help with local travel arrangements. The fact that it was just twenty kilometres from the airport clinched it for her even though it would cost £150 per person per night.

It had crossed Daphne's mind to stay over in the Capital, Bangkok, for a few days before journeying onwards. The group going with her were not particularly well travelled and would probably have a bad impression of Bangkok from the media. The first thing that comes to mind when Bangkok is mentioned is prostitution, Lady Boys and drugs. To make the stop over more inviting Daphne would need to do some research on more cultural activities and maybe some shopping.

To visit a country so far away it would be impractical and exhausting to fit it all into a week. The eager travellers decided that it would have to be a fortnight so that there would be time for sightseeing and maybe a day or two relaxing around the hotel pool. With costs of flights, hotels, meals and excursions it would be a fairly costly holiday. Many of her orchid enthusiast friends were pensioners and for that reason she decided that she would arrange the holiday for a year the following January in order to give them time to save up for the trip.

Daphne was so proud of her beautiful orchids and lived for the times when she could share the love of her hobby with others. She felt that the village flower festival was well worth the hard work and each year they made more profit. It was quickly becoming a lucrative occasion.

Chapter 12

2016 – H.M.Prison Lockwood Park, after the Funeral.

The motion of the van stopping suddenly stirred Louise from her thoughts, the drive back from the funeral had taken longer than it should have done. Traffic was heavy and the many road works made it even worse. Louise was told to sit tight until the gates opened and they were safely inside; obediently, she waited further instructions. There was an ache in the pit of her stomach in anticipation of what was to come; a kind of dread when you know there's no way out of a situation and you just have to endure it whatever happens. There was no conversation between her and the guard as he pulled at her arm to get her out. The large metal security gates hissed as they closed securely behind the vehicle. She walked into the prison that had been her home for the last few months; with many, many more to go. It seemed crazy that she had to be searched before going to her cell as the guards hadn't taken their eyes off her at the funeral, but she was getting used to the formality of prison life and was learning to accept it without question. It was easier that way.

Louise was escorted back to her wing. The smell of the prison had become familiar to her now and bothered her less when compared to the anger and hatred that was shown by one inmate to another on the wing, 'the secure wing'.

Cigarette smoke hung in the acrid air and Louise was reluctant to walk into her cell, a kindly guard poked her back and she stepped forward into the fog. There had been talk that smoking in prison was to be banned as in other Government establishments; the smokers were delighted when the Government decided that prisons were to be the only establishment where smoking was to be allowed and inmates, with the habit, could continue to pollute the air in their cells along with the lungs of their non-smoking cellmates. It was a fact that nearly all prisoners did actually smoke, for some reason it seemed to go with the lifestyle. That fact alone singled Louise out but she had no intention of starting that dreadful habit to be one of the girls. Some of the smoke that hung in the air had a strange sweet odour which was very different to the usual smell of cigarette smoke. Louise slowly began to realise that the sweet smell was an illegal substance that somehow seemed to find its way into the prison and was ignored by the guards for the sake of harmony.

The deafening music blasting from Tracy's radio welcomed Louise as she returned to her 'cosy' little cell for two. The woman she had shared with since her first day on the secure wing didn't look at her as she walked in. Tracy lay on her bed in silence making rings of smoke as she exhaled, listening to the rhythmic banging she called music. The noise offended Louise but she didn't complain. The last time she had past a comment about the music, Tracy flew across the short space between their beds with fists flaying as she spat obscenities an inch from the face of the terrified Louise. Tracy's temper had got her into trouble in the past; it was believed that she had hurt her boyfriend so badly he was hospitalised. The gossip on the wing is rarely wrong but no-one was that keen to get an accurate version enough to actually ask Tracy. Everyone treated her with a distant respect and extreme caution. Louise knew Tracy was a lifer, just like her, so her crime must have been a bad one.

Louise sat on her bed and looked around the cell. It was sparse and grim. Her side of the cell had a few pictures stuck onto the wall, mainly of her Mum and one of them together. There was a large calendar hanging there too with different flowers on each page. Louise loved the page with the orchids. It was the month of June and also her mother's birthday. She had a tear in her eye as she thought about the beautiful orchids her mother had grown and wondered if they were being cared for, now that she was gone. Louise loved to wake each day to the sight of that lovely orchid regardless of the fact that it wasn't June. For some reason that seemed to bother Tracy.

'You've got the wrong date showing again, you idiot.' She'd hiss through her teeth while cigarette smoke streamed out

70

of her flared nostrils. Tracy loved her early morning fix of nicotine.

Louise learned to conform and allow her cellmate to dictate events by the mood she displayed; so she would just change the page on the calendar knowing there was no point trying to explain to someone like Tracy that it reminded her of her mother. Tracy was as hard as nails; fearless, emotionless.

Tracy had been in custody for a long time and knew all the screws, as she called them, always displaying her better side when they were around. Some might call it playing the system, but Louise began to realise that Tracy's bad behaviour to her fellow inmates was her way of telling them to leave well alone. Like Louise, Tracy had no visitors and, in her usual couldn't care less way, showed no concern at being all alone in the world.

It was very different at night on the wing, when the lights were out and all was silent. You could hear the faint, muffled sounds of women crying softly, trying not to be heard. Louise was a light sleeper and the smallest sound would wake her in the dark of night. On many occasions, Tracy would toss and turn in her sleep muttering incoherent sounds; she sounded anxious, almost frightened. Louise would listen intently, eager to make out Tracy's words in an attempt to try and understand her a little better. Something had made her bad. At times like this Louise was confused as to whom the real Tracy actually was; perhaps not the angry person she presented and wanted others to believe she was. Maybe her lifestyle had created the monster she had become and although Louise was fearful of her when she got angry and upset, she had some compassion for her too. An emotion she had learned from her parents in the good times.

Louise was lying quietly on her hard bed, after returning from her mother's funeral; gathering her thoughts and ultimately trying to resign herself to a long future locked up. Not a happy thought but one she would have to endure. She often wondered where her father was and what he was doing. Was he still with Abigail Flint? Or had she left him for someone younger and

71

more handsome? Daphne always said that he'd be left alone and would, one day, want to come home but her bitterness obscured her thoughts of him which made forgiveness impossible. Sometimes, without her mother to dominate her opinions, Louise would occasionally think kindly of him and wonder if he still loved her after all this time. For the most part he had been a good husband and father.

The bell rang out and Louise sat up abruptly. It was the signal telling the prisoners that they could collect their supper from the kitchen. It was always a peaceful and an orderly procedure. The women would make a line and move slowly, in silence, until it was their turn to pick up a tray holding it out, away from their body as they walked though the serving area. The inmates who worked in the kitchen would place the meal on the tray and the women would walk back, in an orderly manner, to their cells to eat in silence. Any problems and their tray would be taken off them by an observing guard and they'd have to go without. The food wasn't bad at all. A menu would be given to everyone to fill in during the day and they could select meals for the following day. There were reasonable choices for each of the three meals they had every day and you could always find something you liked. An employed chef supervised and directed operations in the kitchen but the inmates did the cooking, serving and clearing away. On release from prison some would have a certificate stating the level they had achieved which they could use to find employment on the outside.

Tracy and Louise ate their supper together, in silence. Tracy finished first and put her tray on the floor outside the cell for collection. Louise felt her eyes on her as she took a little longer to finish. No words were spoken and Louise was content that silence was better than friction. But not for long, with an unlit cigarette hanging from the corner of her mouth Tracy spoke.

'Well, Lady Louise, where have you been today?' her head tilted slightly to the left as she lit her cigarette and waited for an answer.

'It was my mother's funeral.' Tracy's face changed, almost showing a little compassion.

'Mothers die. You'll get over it.' She sucked in a long drag from her cigarette and blew it across the cell to Louise as she sat on her bed with the tray on her lap finishing off her supper. Louise really hated that about Tracy; she only ever considered herself. As usual, Louise said nothing. She finished her supper and put the tray out for collection, leaving Tracy to her own miserable company. As she walked to the communal area at the end of the landing she saw some friendly faces. Those chairs and tables were a great escape for Louise; somewhere away from Tracy where you could chat with other prisoners for a short while after supper and before 'lights out'.

'Oh, Louise! How are you? How did the funeral go?' said Amanda. The others looked and waited for her response. Louise didn't think she had any more tears left but here they come again. Maggie got up and put her arms around her. It felt good to Louise. They were her family now. In some ways the other inmates felt maternal towards Louise as she was the youngest on the wing.

Louise tried so hard to adapt to prison life and the types of women incarcerated alongside her. Her cellmate, Tracy, was fairly typical; she had a tough exterior which seemed to be the result of her upbringing and criminal lifestyle. She had developed an impenetrable outer shell of protection under which there seemed to be no sign of a heart. After months together, night and day, Louise knew no more about Tracy than that first day of cell sharing.

The few friends Louise had made at Lockwood Park were Amanda, Maggie and Jan. They never really discussed their crimes but Louise realised that to be on the secure wing they must have done something serious. They seemed perfectly normal people to her; not at all like Tracy and the many others incarcerated along side her. It really was a tough environment to survive in. Women who thought themselves cleverer than the rest were soon brought down to earth, sometimes even beaten until the system of hierarchy was learned and obeyed. There were fights every day.

It was a known fact that the ratio of inmates to guards was growing in the favour of the inmates. Financial cuts were forcing the number of prison guards down to a seriously low level and problems inside the prisons were growing. Even in the women's prisons the guards were assaulted regularly and the fighting between the inmates was escalating to a dangerous level. On occasion there were serious fights which had lead to injury and either a stay in the prison hospital or even a hospital on the outside. On more than one occasion they didn't come back.

When she arrived at the prison, Louise didn't have to tell her fellow prisoners her crime, it was common knowledge. It was in all the papers and on television 'Teenager Murders Married Lover'. It had been a long and drawn out trial and the public wanted blood. In some ways her crime of murder gave her status and Louise accepted graciously, it was easier. There was rarely open discussion about the prisoner's crimes and for that Louise was relieved. Although there were some that enjoyed taunting each other; probably out of boredom.

In the beginning she had heard comments from the mean girls meant for her ears. It made Louise so sad when she heard the hurtful remarks.

'It was', as the French say, 'a Crime of Passion', always accompanied with sarcastic laughter from the other women.

After a while the ridicule eased off and she got on with making a life for herself inside. At night before she went to sleep she'd say a silent prayer and hoped that God would understand that it was impossible to speak the words out loud. She would pray in silence for forgiveness from God for all the bad things she had done, and for understanding from those who had turned their back on her. Above all she prayed for help to sustain herself in the horror of prison life and to keep her safe until she was free again; whenever that would be. She always whispered the word Amen, hoping that Tracy would not hear her.

The night of the funeral Louise found it hard to settle. She lay on the thin, mattress waiting for 'lights out' breathing in the pungent, disgusting air of Tracy's stale cigarette smoke which had no escape from this almost airtight cell.

The lights went out suddenly, without notice. The cell was grey but not in total darkness. Her barred windows allowed in some light from a crescent moon. She felt the tears burn as she closed her eyes and imagined her bedroom back home at the vicarage. Her sweet scented room with the pink, heart-shaped string of lights hanging from the ceiling and all things familiar. Her mother and father in the next room sleeping or talking quietly about their day. This would never be again.

The way Louise's simple life had become so complicated had caused such hurt and irreparable damage to those she loved. Her beloved Alex, gone forever. Her one true love but the husband of another. His body placed in a coffin and burned in a cremation ceremony. For some reason Susannah had allowed his parents to take him home to his beloved Wales. Instead of allowing Louise to grieve, they incarcerated her for the crime of his murder. The burden was too great for her mother to bear and she took her own life, leaving Louise alone and afraid. Nothing could ever be the same again and she couldn't put it right. Exhaustion engulfed her as she fell into a deep, merciful sleep; dreaming herself to a better place.

And so life went on at Her Majesty's Prison Lockwood Park. The same old routine day after day and the silence of the night with only her thoughts and fears for company. No letters, no visitors, just waiting and waiting, for nothing.

Louise tried hard to keep out of the troubles that could suddenly blow up on the wing. She had learned to read situations and remove herself before they became volatile and involve her.

Tracy had decided one day to venture out of her cell and sit at a table on the landing; this was a particularly unusual thing for her to do, she never left the cell. Louise's friend Amanda was sitting at the table alone and spoke to Tracy.

'It's good to see you out of your cell Tracy. You must get bored in there all day.' If anyone could get some response from Tracy it was Amanda; she was one of the nicer ones.

'What's it to you, whore?'

'I'm just pleased to see you Tracy, nothing more.' Amanda answered ignoring the insult.

They sat in silence for a while. One of the cell doors nearby opened and Tracy got up and went in. The door closed behind her and Amanda was left alone again. Within a few minutes Tracy came back onto the landing and went straight into her own cell where Louise was reading; shutting the heavy door behind her. It was impossible to stay in the cell with the door closed, Louise knew Tracy would light a cigarette and she'd had enough of her selfish ways. Getting off her bed to open the door Louise felt a pull on the back of her head and she was dragged to the floor. She tried to fight Tracy off but she had a firm grip on Louise's long red hair.

'Leave the door closed, you bitch; I've got things to do.' She let go of Louise's hair and sat back on her bed. Louise did the same. It wasn't a good time to argue with Tracy; Louise had learned not to aggravate an already volatile situation.

'I need something, you know, to help me.' Tracy was shaking.

'What do you mean?' Louise was slowing getting the message.

'I need a special smoke and I don't want the screws smell it; they've warned me to be more discrete. Know what I mean?'

'I think so.' Louise began to realise Tracy had some cannabis from one of the dealers on the wing. It was common for things to be bought and sold amongst the inmates and Louise was learning just how much of this was going on.

'Don't you grass me up or it will be bad for you, and Jan will be after your blood too.'

'Jan? You got it from Jan?'

'She's no angel, Lady Louise! Wise up!'

Louise was shocked to hear that Jan had drugs. She had realised early on in her sentence that there were drugs to be had, but never thought Jan would be so reckless. Everything began to fall into place. Jan always had extras that others didn't, like shower gel, soap, chocolate and cigarettes. Louise thought her job in the kitchen was funding the items but she always seemed to have more than most.

With all these revelations coming out she felt stupid and used; was Amanda and Maggie involved too?

Tracy lit up her 'special cigarette' and Louise left the cell, remembering to close the door tightly behind her.

Amanda was still sitting alone on the landing and Louise joined her.

'You know, don't you?' Amanda looked straight at Louise watching her reaction.

'You know about the spliff?'

'What?' said Louise.

'The spliff. The cannabis spliff?'

'Yes I do. It was from Jan.'

'Listen Louise. Don't think badly of Jan. You know how hard things can be in this place, and if a few nice things make it easier, then so be it.'

'But Jan is one of the nice ones, she's my friend.'

'You really are a child, aren't you?' Amanda gave a cynical laugh. 'I sometimes wonder where you got the balls to kill your lover from, although I must admit you've earned respect for it.'

'What's that got to do with Jan drug dealing?' Louise was getting annoyed with Amanda but not enough to pour out the truth about her version of her offence and have everyone laugh at her.

'It's our life Lou. We didn't have a life like yours. We had to fight for everything we needed and take the rest.' It was hard for Amanda to make Louise understand things that she'd never seen or felt.

'In our world we sometimes need a little something to ease the pain and make the bad things go away.'

'You take it too?'

Amanda didn't answer, there was no need, and her silence told Louise the truth.

'And Maggie?'

Again no response.

Louise felt even more alone. There was nowhere to hide now, no-one to run to. She walked back to her cell where Tracy lay on her bed smoking her spliff. Louise was quickly becoming part of the deceit as she closed the door behind her keeping the smell of the cannabis in and ran to the stainless steel toilet behind a small partition and emptied the contents of her stomach into the pan.

After a minute or two she flushed and went to lie down on her bed. There was nothing left to do.

'Do you want a drag? It'll make you feel nice, fancy pants.'

'No thanks.'

Louise turned her face to the wall and closed her eyes. She wanted to get out of that place more than ever now so that she wouldn't have to get involved with all this nastiness. Remembering her day in court when the judge had decided on her sentence she relived his words.

'For the offence of murder, I have only one option before me. You have pleaded your innocence throughout the trial but ultimately you have been found guilty of the shooting of your married lover, Alexander Rhydian Turner. No remorse at any time has been shown by you. It is because of you that his widow is left alone to raise their child without a father and his parents heartbroken at the loss of their son. You are therefore sentenced to life imprisonment with no concession which, in your case, means you serve no less than fifteen years. When you are released you will spend the remainder of your sentence of life imprisonment, on licence. Go with the officers, Miss Anderson.'

With nearly fifteen years left to serve in this place Louise had to have a purpose, an aim. She had been told that once settled there would be opportunities of things to do to fill her day. She was ready; tomorrow she would ask for more information. Louise felt she had lost the friendship of Amanda, Maggie and Jan and was now totally alone. Her mind was focussed on the remainder of her time in custody and she was determined not to waste another second of it. She had to learn how to become strong and to survive.

Louise had a sleepless night but in a way she was excited. She would ask what jobs were available on her wing and maybe get some form of education; she had seen films where prisoners get out of jail totally reformed with a Law degree or the like. It brought a cynical smile to her face.

There was a wooden box fixed to the wall on every wing with a table underneath with forms on and a pencil chained to the table. Louise had seen them before but not really taken any notice; today she read one. It said that if a prisoner wanted to speak with an official then a form must be filled in accordingly.

There were boxes to be ticked and a space to write a short sentence with reasons why she was requesting to speak with a member of the Independent Monitoring Board. Louise completed it in a few minutes. She folded it small enough to be pushed through the slot at the top of the box. All she had to do now was wait.

Surprisingly it didn't take long for a lady to come to her wing and ask to speak with her. She arrived the following afternoon; Louise was surprised that she wasn't an employee of the Prison Service and didn't wear a uniform. The lady worked in a voluntary capacity and gave her time to the prison to see that fair play was shown to both the inmates and the officers in charge. Her role was explained clearly to Louise; she would gather the information and the senior administration manager of the prison would make arrangements to interview her.

The lady was easy to speak with.

'What is it you want to do, Louise?'

'I'd like to continue my education so that I will have some hope of getting a job when I get out of here.'

'That's a very mature point of view, Louise. What were you studying before you came here?'

'I had just passed two 'A' levels in Accountancy and Law Miss.'

'What grades did you get Louise?'

'A in Accounting and B in Law, Miss.'

'Very good. However, as much as I would like to I can't really promise anything but I'll certainly ask someone to come and speak with you about your choices. Of course there is always the library in the meantime. You can borrow the appropriate books and get started on your own. That will also prove you are determined. It may help them to make a favourable decision.'

'I will, Miss. Thank you very much.'

Louise could feel the woman's empathy towards her; it was comforting.

It took almost a week but a man finally turned up on the wing and Louise was taken to a small room to be interviewed by him. He introduced himself as Mr Leatherby and had a file with him which told him all about Louise. Thumbing through the pages of the file, he spoke to Louise without lifting his head.

'I see you have been well educated, leaving school with 'A' Level Accounting, grade A and 'A' Level Law, grade B. I have made some notes as to what I would suggest you do with your time here at Lockwood Park. I hope you agree.' It didn't seem by his manner that Louise would be allowed to disagree. Louise was hoping to tell Mr Leatherby what she had in mind but that wasn't going to happen. His decision seemed to be a foregone conclusion, of sorts. So she just listened attentively.

'I believe the best type of work for you would be in the prison library. It's simple work although mostly solitary. There is an outside volunteer in charge and you would simply do as you are told. Along with that you may continue your qualifications in either Law or Accounting. The choice would be yours and you would have some sort of written diploma or even a degree at the end of it. The degree would be with The Open University, if that's what you decide, and you may well know that you can attain the same standard or level that you would if you were to attend daily at a university outside. Any questions so far?'

He looked at Louise and could see she was keeping up with him so he continued.

'You will receive a small salary of £3.00 each week for your work in the library and, of course, the education side of the programme would be free to you as part of your rehabilitation and to assist the smooth running of your resettlement at the end of your sentence. Any questions?'

'I don't think so.'

'Good, you can start in the library tomorrow and will be advised of the rest in due course. Good day.'

'Thank you, Sir.'

They left the room together; Louise went back to her cell and Mr Leatherby to his office.

Chapter 13

2014 – Alex and Louise Grow Closer.

The problem with Louise as she reached puberty was that she showed little or no interest in the opposite sex; young, handsome young boys of her own age to be exact. She had friends, and friends that were boys but the other girls had more of a desire to have them as boyfriends; which set Louise apart. She would sometimes have a night out with a mixed group of school friends and, as most teenagers do, they would pair up. Louise ultimately avoided these situations and eventually went out less and less. The boys of her age were boring and childish as far as Louise was concerned. She believed she'd gain more by working hard in school; of course, this was preferred and encouraged by her mother. Now that it was just the two of them, Daphne wanted her only child close and protected in every way; which, in her naivety, she believed to be right and proper. It was clear to all who knew them well that their closeness was becoming more obsessive and their shield of emotional protection becoming impenetrable. They had joined ranks against the world since George had left and they had become more dependent on each other daily.

The problems started when Alex and Susannah moved to Camberley Edge. Louise was in awe of him in every way and blossomed under his attention. She felt that Susannah neglected him and was spending too much time away from home, hence deserving whatever came her way. Since the couple had set up home in Camberley Edge, Louise called into Jasmine Cottage at every opportunity to see Alex; she had become besotted by him. Not long after they had met each other, one of their many conversations was his work in the city and when Louise discovered what he had done for a living she couldn't believe her luck. Like his wife, he was a qualified solicitor and as one of Louise's 'A' Level subjects was Law she asked him to help. So on the evenings that Susannah was on call at the apartment in

London the pair would work together in the cosiness of Alex's front room.

Daphne had secured a position for Louise, after completing her 'A' levels, in an accountancy firm that she had worked for before marrying George. The firm was in the village and therefore near home, so, even though Daphne had talked to Louise about her going to University they had decided that it was far better for her to remain close to home. As usual, it was Daphne that did most of the talking and Louise just listened and agreed with her mother. One of the partners of L & J Thomas Associates who gave Louise the opportunity of a job had been a friend of Daphne's for many years. It had been clear all those years ago that the senior partner was sweet on the lovely Daphne as an attractive lady but the admiration was not reciprocated. Even then, Daphne only had eyes for George. For old times sake Louise was offered a position in the firm.

Louise was pleased that there was no pressure from her mother to go to University she knew in her heart that Alex was to be hers one day and she needed to be around to ensure the relationship flourished; albeit undercover.

With Susannah away working every day and staying over at night in their London apartment more and more, the stage was set. It was on one of Susannah's away nights that it all happened. Whether there was unconscious intent or not will never be known but Louise went home straight from school that night and decided she would change out of her uniform into jeans and T shirt. Alex noticed when he opened the door to her.

'Hi Louise, you are looking nice. Are you going somewhere special?'

'No. I went home to drop off my books, so I thought I'd change.' She was almost apologetic in her manner.

'Well, you look lovely.'

Alex seemed to see something in Louise, perhaps he saw and felt her adoration for him and was flattered. They were an improbable couple but it certainly seemed that their relationship was more than simply friendship.

'I thought I'd take the dogs for a run in the fields before it rains.'

Louise looked upwards and indicated to the black clouds in the distance.

'I think I'll come too.' His response put Louise in seventh heaven.

They walked together to the far corner of the field behind the house and let the dogs off their leashes for a run. As Louise and Alex walked side by side along the narrow boundary path he touched her hand gently and waited for some kind of reaction. Smiling, she consensually slipped her hand into his. The long awaited moment had arrived and Louise couldn't catch her breath.

Over the months, Alex had got to know Louise quite well and he began to see the woman behind the girls face. There was something that others missed and he found it tantalisingly attractive. She paid him the attention he need and it made him feel so good. Louise always listened intently when he talked and loved his dogs as much as he did. He saw her sweetness, her honesty but more importantly he recognised her infatuation with him. With a few relationships behind him he had learned to recognise the signs and where Louise was concerned it was a red flashing light. Barely a woman but his for the taking.

'You have become so important to me, sweet Louise.'

The moment had come. Alex took Louise in his arms. Her heart beat so fast, she felt she might faint. He pulled her closer and it felt so right. As their lips gently touched, the heavens opened and it poured with rain. Reluctantly, they separated; calling the dogs they ran back to the house, laughing. Even the rain couldn't spoil that moment and what was to come.

Alex put the dogs in the out building and ran into the house after Louise. They were soaked through.

'Go up to the bathroom and get out of those wet clothes Lou, there are robes hanging behind the door.' Louise obeyed and came downstairs in a white robe, presumably Susannah's.

Alex had poured two large brandies and handed one to the shivering girl.

'Don't go telling your mother that I'm giving you alcohol. Of course, it's purely medicinal.' He gave her the sweetest smile and knew she was his. Louise didn't like the taste of the brandy but drank every drop as per Alex's instructions. Then he made his move. Taking her hand he pulled her up off the sofa and into his arms. Louise had never been kissed like that before and her head swam with excitement. The next thing they knew they were in the marital bed and sweet Louise had given her virginity to Alex. For her it was the best day of her life and one she would always remember. Alex was sensitive and respectful; he said all the right things. They lay together for a long time in silence afterwards. Louise shed a silent tear of happiness and Alex seemed to fall asleep.

An hour or so later Alex woke with a start.

'Your mother will be worried about you my darling.' Alex whispered in her ear.

'I can't bear to leave you, Alex.'

'There will be more, my sweet, I promise,' he whispered and gently smoothed her hair from her face.

And there were more, many, many more times under the ruse of dog walking or helping with studies and the like. Louise was most definitely in love and this whole affair meant the world to her with expectations of marriage and a lifetime together. At night, alone in her bed she would dream of a life in the village with Alex. People would forget the sordid side of their deception and see how much in love they were; forgiving them their sins. He would, of course, have to divorce Susannah, but she could live in the London apartment so that Louise could move into the house with Alex as Mrs Alexander Turner.

The transition from lover to wife turned out to be a slower process than Louise would have liked; in fact there was no movement at all. Alex had never exactly told Louise that he loved her but she believed that his desire to see her meant the same thing. Neither did he take part in the conversations that Louise often initiated regarding their future together. On the other hand, he didn't contradict her in any way which seemed to Louise that he was in agreement. Alex was playing with fire.

They had their special times together whilst Susannah worked and Alex was content with that. Louise decided to play the game for the time being and was very careful to have good reasons for her visits to Jasmine Cottage; at the same time bursting for the moment she could tell all. Alex was happy with their arrangements and oblivious to Louise's obsessive infatuation. If he hadn't been so involved with his building project, keeping his wife happy and his adulterous affair he may have noticed how dangerous the whole situation was becoming.

On rare occasions Louise would reflect and remember what Abigail Flint, the tart, had done to her mother. This was different of course; she and Alex were in love. Her father couldn't possibly have loved Abigail the way she loved Alex.

So life continued in Camberley Edge. Alex spent hours on the new kennels he was building, mostly alone to save money. A large central building where he could train the gundogs in bad weather and a separate building with kennels for the dogs to sleep. The other building would be the most expensive not only to build but to fit out with heat lamps and various equipment needed for the breeding of pups they could eventually sell. Alex was planning to keep some of the pups and train them as gun dogs to a high standard with a view to selling them on fully trained. He loved the boisterous, energetic temperament of the Spaniels. They would flush out the prey for the attack. The eager yet more laid back attitude of the Labrador Retrievers that knew how to be patient and wait for their master's command to retrieve. His plans were grand and Alex was prepared for the hard work to get the project off its feet. Not for a second did Louise have a place in all this. It was always Susannah.

It would be fair to say that Susannah was passive as far as Alex's dreams were concerned; her role was mainly to fund the business until it made its own money. As soon as they were in profit Susannah had provisionally agreed to retire from work and live the country life. That, at least, was the plan.

Louise, on the other hand, loved to hear all about her lover's plans and dreams. Hanging on his every word and giving him the encouragement he lacked from his wife. Most of the time Alex kept his mind trained on the task ahead giving little thought to the love struck Louise. It was always Susannah in his thoughts when he dreamed of being a country gent with a wife and children. He never contradicted Louise when she talked about her dream of life together but expected that one day she would move on, finding a boy of her own age to love. That was Alex's misguided belief.

For Alex, Jasmine Cottage was to be the fulfilment of a dream away from the city lights. Life in London had been fast and for the most part it had been fun. It was so very different to the life he had know in Llandrindod Wells and the Welsh family farm. City life had held an excitement that Alex loved at first but for him it became unsustainable and he began to long for a more moderate lifestyle. He was confused and even vulnerable when Louise had come into his life; he often had feelings of guilt knowing that she wanted a future with him and one day he would think of a way to let her down gently, to tell her it was over between them. It would never be easy to hurt the sweet Louise but he loved Susannah with a passion and his future was definitely with her. He believed that Louise would understand.

Alex's life had its very own melting pot. The woman he adored and admired, Susannah. The young girl who gave him the love and attention he longed for, Louise. Then there were his dreams of building his own business, the only thing he was truly working at. The problem was they were an explosive mix and one day he would have to choose. Alex was a kind person but his lack of focus and control over his life was building and escalating into an unimaginable disaster. He believed that Louise would understand that they really had no future yet never made that clear to her. A teenager in love, with the belief that her man would do anything for her was perhaps ignorant; but the signs were there. Louise had told him the story of her father's affair and desertion with a younger woman. Bells should have been ringing loud and clear in Alex's head.

As a boy growing up on the farm in Wales Alex had had a few girlfriends but it seems he had learned nothing about the opposite sex. As soon as he realised there was a chance to escape the farming life and have an academic education his mind became focused on his school work and every night he read and read and read. Only on rare occasions did he venture out with his brothers to enjoy himself. Occasionally enjoying the company of a girl who had her eye on him and made it easy for him to get what he wanted with little effort on his part. Alex would have a few one night stands but his school work always came first and he simply didn't understand the hurt and confusion he caused to these young girls.

This time it would be Louise.

Chapter 14

2008 - London Firm of Solicitors.

Alex Turner and Susannah Hopkins had met when they both joined a large partnership of solicitors in the city of London. As newcomers to the firm, they were given the 'not so interesting' jobs that were put to one side by the senior solicitors in the firm for the beginners to gain their basic experience on, a system practiced in many companies and of which the couple were compliant, acknowledging the inevitable. The friendship between the couple grew and their business life soon overlapped into their private lives.

Susannah had come from a family of solicitors in Kent, but thought her life should be in London where she believed the action was, both night and day. Susannah was fun loving to put it mildly. Her father had offered her a place in the family firm alongside himself, her younger brother and a few junior members of the group. Susannah, however, had more far reaching ideas and ambitions. Alex was in awe of her. She was confident and turned heads when she walked down the street. A striking beauty with long blonde hair and extremely long legs that she displayed with grace and elegance, she would blend in well on the catwalk. Not only was she beautiful, she was extremely clever. Her father believed in his daughter and knew there were no limits even to the point of being the first judge in the Hopkins family if she put the work in. Susannah had it all and confidence as well.

Alex, on the other hand had a completely different background and upbringing. He was brought up on a farm and it had been supposed that he would follow that line. The farm was just outside a small town in mid-Wales called Llandrindod Wells. This, redbrick, town was very popular in Victorian times when visitors came from miles around for the healing waters that supposedly cured ailments. Whether the waters actually were healing really didn't matter too much because the belief and expectations of the visitors brought a good income into the town. Many salubrious hotels were built to accommodate these people, bringing jobs to the area which made the hoteliers very happy and extremely rich. Lland'od, as it's known locally, is in such a beautiful part of Wales with the rolling hills dotted with farms. From a distance, the hills look as if there are cotton wool balls walking slowly over them but, of course, that's the famous Welsh sheep. Other animals were farmed, but it's always the sheep that visitors remembered.

Alex loved to tell Louise about his childhood and the freedom he knew growing up on the farm.

'You would truly love Wales, Lou. Wales is renowned for its rainfall. Low clouds and high mountains equate to rainfall and Wales has its fair share. But there's something magical about it. Without the rain the grass wouldn't be green. It has some of the most incredibly fertile landscapes as a direct result of the climate. Other benefits of the precipitation is the arable farmland. Not forgetting the well fed cows and famous sheep that enjoy the freedom of the Welsh hills. Flocks of sheep roam the mountainside and enjoy a good life until they end up as a Sunday Roast accompanied by a good helping of mint sauce. There's nothing quite like Welsh lamb, Lou.'

Louise always listened intently to the stories Alex loved to tell.

'Then why did you go to London, Alex? If you love Wales as much as you say, perhaps you should have become a farmer like your dad.'

'I wanted to see what life was like in the big city. I knew that my only chance of that was to work hard and to go further with my education, hopefully making something of myself. I don't regret it. It made me what I am today.'

'Perhaps you'll go back one day, Alex.'

Alex couldn't help himself, he continued.

'Did I tell you about the town of Lland'od? It was built around a large square that's used for festivals and fairs. Each and every year the town celebrate Victorian Week where locals and visitors alike dress up in Victorian-style clothing. There is entertainment in most of the hotels and guest speakers entertain the crowds. The green on the square has a fun fair and stalls selling crafts, furniture and food to name but a few. All year round the hotels are busy with visitors who come to see the local sights and the beautiful countryside. In Victorian times the visitors would come to take the waters but now they come to see things of interest like the Elan Valley Dam which stores water, not least for Wales. The beautiful lake within reach of the town centre and many more tourist attractions. Wherever you are in Wales you are never far from the lovely, sandy beaches which also draw the crowds. I'll take you there one day.'

The suggestion of going to the place Alex grew up made Louise happy and hopeful. For that reason she always wanted to know more about his childhood. It made her feel closer to him, more secure.

Having been brought up in a home with three generations living there, Alex was understandably missing the family chats and evenings together. He would never have believed he'd miss the family as much as he did. But he had Louise now and that helped.

'How did you make the move to London and your life in law?'

'I obviously had to work hard in school. After my 'A' levels I applied to the Westminster Law School in London and to my amazement I was accepted. I was the very first lawyer-to-be in the Turner family. It was long and hard but I then graduated and found myself a job at a large law firm called Benjamin, Scott, Walters and Parsons. I was so proud. I thought I'd made it.'

Alex carefully omitted to say Susannah also worked there. In fact they joined the firm together.

Susannah, the supreme party animal who led Alex into a world of extremes at night. She was known mostly because of her father and his reputation as a leading barrister and was welcomed by the elite members of London's night life. What she earned she spent; mainly on designer shoes and bags. Alex had been carried along in the affluent and frivolous lifestyle so very different to his own. Their hedonistic way of life was like a drug and there was never enough.

By day the couple worked hard to learn the ways of the practice. They slowly but surely moved up the ladder. Mr Benjamin seemed to have an eye for Susannah and gave her the opportunities perhaps more appropriate to her family background. It became clear to Alex that there were conversations between Mr Benjamin and Mr Hopkins, Susannah's dad. Maybe a little nepotism but there was nothing he could do about it so he went along with everything that was asked of him in the hope that he would prove his worth by hard work and effort.

Alex recalled that year of busy courtship and when he asked Susannah to move into his flat.

'I don't think so darling, where would I put my shoes?' she had laughed. 'What if we put a little more cash into the kitty and buy something nice?' So Alex took out a loan for his half and 'daddy' gave Susannah hers. They had been very happy for the most part. When they were alone Susannah was sweet and kind. It was only when her friends came around or they went out on the town that she became an extrovert. Alex had put up with it because he loved her and knew it was all for show.

They had shopped together for sofas, a bed and all the things that would make their new flat a home, the result was amazing, but had been mostly down to Susannah. The couple were climbing the ladder with home ownership and racing up the ladder of employment success. Life was good, albeit exhausting.

Susannah had been working hard at honing her knowledge of criminal law under the supervision of one of the partners, Philip Scott. Phil was the youngest partner at forty but was keen and he was quickly building an excellent reputation for himself as one of London's sharpest defence advocates. Susannah spent many days in court observing Phil in readiness for her time. There were drawbacks in criminal law, it wasn't nine to five. Criminals worked all hours and if arrested at night their lawyer would be expected to attend the police station and still be at work the following day.

Phil had been covering nearly all the crime work of the partnership and although financially rewarding it played havoc with his bachelor, social life. He constantly complained to Byron, the practice manager who had been with the company from the beginning but old Mr Benjamin held the reigns firmly. Eventually Byron convinced the old man that a young lady would raise the profile of the practice in more ways than one. Susannah turned out to fit that profile exactly and when, after a settling in period, Susannah showed a keen interest the deed was almost done. Unlike many before her she showed that she had an edge; an assertiveness that gave her the power and confidence needed in the courtroom.

It wasn't long before the opportunity arrived and Susannah had her first case to manage, alone. She was superb and earned the respect she deserved. Work came in hard and fast thereafter; her career took off.

Alex had watched with pride as Susannah became part of the criminal team of Phil and Susannah and knew she would fly in the partnership. He understood that his conveyance work would never be as exciting, but he enjoyed working for Benjamin, Scott, Walters and Parsons and the work he did was bread & butter for the firm; houses were always being bought and sold.

Ever since he was a child on the farm in Wales, Alex knew he would make a life somewhere else. He didn't know how or where until he found his ability lay in learning and understanding in the world of academia. His clarity of thinking and ability to focus stood him apart from his peers in the classroom. Life on the farm wasn't for Alex and that suited the family. His brothers would eventually take over the running of the family business when their parents retired and the boys would, no doubt, marry and have children. It would be untenable to try and support three families so they let Alex go.

His adventure had begun.

Chapter 15

August 2009 – Alex Takes Susannah to Wales.

Although his job at the firm kept him busy, Alex would sometimes feel a little homesick for the peace and tranquillity of the farm and have the need to go home for a short visit. It had always been his intention to take Susannah with him so that he could introduce her to the family. He also had a surprise for her in the shape of a two carat diamond engagement ring, set in Welsh gold of course. Where else would he propose to the woman he loved other than the mountains of home?

With arguments challenged and his firmness overruling any objections Susannah had for going, they had set off after work and arrived at the farm late on the Friday evening just as the summer sun was falling behind the western mountains and into the sea beyond. The welcome she received from the family showed Susannah that Alex's perseverance was worthwhile. They had a light supper and early to bed in readiness for the grand tour she would be given in the morning.

A packed lunch prepared by Alex' Mam was almost too heavy to carry but they put it in the boot of the car and set off. Alex was apprehensive as he had planned to propose at the lake before going home early evening and was praying the weather would be favourable.

They set off in glorious sunshine. The journey to Aberystwyth was first on the agenda. Alex explained to Susannah the importance of 'kicking the bar' at the end of the promenade for luck. Important to him but apparently not to Susannah, however, she went along with it to please Alex. The sun was warm and the forecast good so they moved on to Borth beach for their picnic, just a few miles away and a nicer, more tranquil beach than Aberystwyth. Susannah slowly began to see how all this was so important to Alex. He took great pleasure in showing her his childhood and the things he did with his family; he wanted to share. She began to enjoy the experience and allowed herself to become part of it. It dawned on her that she didn't have memories like these. Her life had been pomp and splendour with extravagance being the main ingredient. As Alex spoke, Susannah lay back onto the rug that he'd brought from the car for the picnic and listened for the first time. She liked what she heard.

After a lazy lunch they lay together on the warm sand talking and dozing, they even ventured into the cold sea for a paddle but not for long. Alex had something important on his mind and was desperate for it to go well.

'Come on. Let's make a move. I want you to see the Elan Dam before the lake.' Alex packed away the remains of the picnic and ushered Susannah back into the car.

'Darling, can we do the lake tomorrow? I am so tired; you've worn me out with your adventures.'

'Mam will expect us to spend the day with them tomorrow and I can't take you back to London tomorrow evening without a visit to the dam and the lake,' he kissed her cheek gently and she gladly conceded.

The Elan Valley Dam took very little time. They took a few pictures, mainly of Susannah peering over the edge with a look of terror on her face when she saw the drop. Then moved quickly on to the lake, back at Llandrindod Wells.

As they got out of the car near the shop and restaurant Alex took Susannah's hand and they walked in silence to the other side of the lake. It really was quite beautiful in the evening sun and everything was perfect, just as Alex had hoped. As luck would have it there was no-one on the far side of the lake and a perfect place for romance.

Alex stopped suddenly and stood in front of Susannah, taking both her hands in his.

'I love you so much Susannah. You are my life and my future,' he slipped down on one knee before she could work out what was happening and took the ring box out of his pocket. Susannah suddenly realised and felt light headed but so happy.

'Will you be my wife?' Alex had a tear in his eye.

'I will. Of course, I will,' she almost shouted. Alex slipped the ring on her finger and kissed her with the tenderness of a man who would love and cherish this woman until the day he dies.

Little did Alex know that the day he dies would be sooner rather than later.

The journey home from Llandrindod Wells to London was long and hard, even for a Sunday evening. They both fell into bed exhausted leaving their unpacked bags for another time. Alex didn't even hear Susannah getting up on the Monday morning for work; he was so tired from the journey he overslept. At times like this the difference in the couple's character was clear; Susannah was driven, Alex definitely not! The ambition that Alex had was to achieve the usual things in life; a wife to love and share his life, a nice home, cars, 2.4 children and the job needed to sustain such a lifestyle. Susannah, on the other hand, wanted 'all of the above' but without a recognised end. She had been raised in a family of successful lawyers and, not only was it expected of her, but she wanted to be the best she could be. Susannah wanted to be recognised in the world of law as being one of the best, getting rich would be a by product but essential all the same. There was a lot of assuming between the couple. They believed they wanted the same but there were major differences. It may even be possible that Alex didn't really know what he wanted, though he thought he did. It might have saved the heartbreak that came later if they had only communicated more.

As Alex awoke and realised that Susannah had left for the office without him; he made the conscious decision not to rush. In fact he sat and enjoyed some fresh coffee then rang home to speak with his mother.

'Bore da, Mam,' his salutation was an unexpected surprise to his mother.

'Are you alright, son?' she questioned.

'Oh yes Mam, I just thought I'd ring and thank you for a lovely weekend. Susannah was delighted.'

'I am pleased cariad. She's a lovely girl.'

They chatted for a while until Alex decided it was time to leave for work and face the day ahead. He showered and donned his usual grey three piece suit. Looking the part, he made the journey to his office.

Susannah, with Phil's help, was defending in a contest which was expected to last for a few days. They would be engrossed in the twists and turns that this type of trial would experience so Alex knew that he should leave well alone and give them a wide berth.

Having dealt with a few matters that were waiting on his desk and checking his diary for the coming week Alex left the office around six p.m. with no sign of Susannah and Phil. He arrived home before 7 pm and got started on a beef lasagne for dinner, Su's favourite.

It must have been after 8 o'clock when the phone rang and Alex heard Susannah's voice on the other end.

'Hi Babe, sorry I'm late, Phil and I are at the office. There are a few unexpected problems that we have to deal with before we go back into court tomorrow.'

Before Alex could speak Susannah continued.

'Don't wait for me to eat with you darling; Phil and I have picked up some food on the way back from court.'

Although disappointed, what else could Alex say? 'OK love, see you later.'

He didn't tell her that he'd made lasagne and had her favourite Merlot waiting. Sitting for a while feeling a little sorry for himself he decided that it would be such a waste to leave the already opened Merlot and, in no time, the empty bottle was in the bin. A drunken Alex went to bed and didn't even hear Susannah get home.

That formed the pattern of their life together. Alex was content to see Susannah grow and develop into one of the most sought after defence advocates on the circuit. On the other hand he was beginning to have some worrying feelings and second thoughts about his own career. Putting the feelings down to feeling a little homesick, Alex resolved to get on with his life and future.

Chapter 16

2017 - H.M. Prison Lockwood Park.

Louise was not coping well with her incarceration. There were times when arguments and fights on the wing got so bad she would have gladly taken her life, had she the ability to do so. The thought of years in prison was more than she could bear. Louise was a novice at this criminal lifestyle and, on times, things would get so bad that she would prefer to stay in her cell with Tracy. Prison life is what is expected of it. Unpleasant. An accepting frame of mind would cope with the situation more easily, or even a plan.

Louise developed a plan to cope with her life inside, and it did work to a point. She had been working in the prison library for over a year and had begun her Open University Law course. But her dark days were hard to get through, and the nights even worse.

Because of her stand against Jan, and her drug dealing, she became more isolated. Her belief in right was making her life untenable so she made a decision to back down and offer Jan an olive branch.

'No time like the present.' She thought.

It was about an hour before 'lights out' and she knew the girls would be at the tables on the landing. She was nervous but intent in making amends and life easier for herself.

As she walked towards the group she heard Amanda say. 'Look who's coming.'

'Jan, can I have a word?' Her voice was a little shaky.

'What about, Lou?'

'You and me.' Louise tried to smile.

Jan got up from her seat and walked towards Louise. Her face was grim but Louise knew Jan was a good person and just wanted to get it overwith.

When Jan got close Louise spoke.

'Jan, I'm sorry for the way I've been. You know, about the spliff. It's not my place to judge you, we're all the same in here and how we get by is our own business.'

Jan just looked at Louise. The apology didn't seem to be working and Louise was getting more nervous.

To Louise's relief Jan put her arms around her.

'You're just a kid with a lot to learn and you'll learn it all in here.'

Louise was so pleased she burst into tears. Jan slipped her arm through Louise's and led her to the tables.

Jan tapped Amanda on the shoulder.

'Lady Louise needs that chair more than you.'

Amanda got up immediately so that Louise could sit down. They all laughed together. Maybe Louise was beginning to understand the way things worked inside.

The apology certainly took the pressure off a heated situation.

After working in the library each day, Louise was given permission to study there for her law degree with the Open University. Tracy would never have given her peace and quiet in the cell and she had a large table in the library to work on.

Time went by slowly at Lockwood Park. Studying kept her focussed and she lived for the day she would walk out and into the world, albeit alone.

Chapter 17

2011 - Alex and Susannah Marry in Style.

The wedding date was set and the time drew closer, the happy couple were drawn into the growing excitement of their special day. They forgot the troubles of life as lawyers and looked forward to a rosy future together; life was pretty perfect. It was expected that they would marry at the family home in Kent. Why not? It was better than any hotel and there were staff ready and willing to do what was expected of them. The house had been in the family for generations and improved with each. As third great grandfather to Susannah, William Hopkins had bought it the nineteenth century when Victoria ruled the land. As was Hopkins family tradition, each first born son was named William which made Susannah's father the fourth William and her brother the fifth.

Susannah's parents were delighted that their only daughter was marrying Alex; they had got to know him over the months and adored him. Mr and Mrs Hopkins believed it was the perfect match and they loved the fact that he was in the legal profession. The wedding plans were well under control and that was due to Isabel Hopkins' hard work. Susannah didn't have much time to help but supervised from afar; checking from time to time that her mother was following the details they had agreed on.

William and Isabel had not met Alex's parents and had no idea what to expect. Alex had told them that Bryn and Shan were farmers and their younger sons, James and Edward, were due to take over the farm when Bryn made the decision that they were ready and competent enough to do so. Shan wanted that day to come more quickly than Bryn.

It had been agreed by all that the Turner's would stay at the Hopkins mansion the night before and the night of the wedding, after all there was plenty of room.

The journey from Lland'od to Kent wasn't a good one; mainly down to Bryn.

Bryn had never needed satellite navigation in Lland'od and it wasn't a feature of his ten year old car anyway, so the boys gave directions from the back seat with the help of a very old map. Bryn also used his natural directional intuition which was contrary to the map and caused a few arguments between the navigators and the driver. As usual Shan sat in silence and let the men get on with it which worked out eventually.

As the old car neared the outskirts of the village the boys put away the map and relied on Alex's hand written drawing. For a lawyer Alex hadn't done a bad job of the pencilled map, even marking the roadsides with pubs and shops along the way, which is always helpful if only to ensure you are on the right road. When they came to the entrance of the house Bryn stopped the car and took the map to confirm it was the right place. He was expecting grandeur but this was off the scale. The front of the car was facing the enormous entrance gates and before Bryn new it a voice was welcoming them from somewhere; there was no one to be seen.

'Good afternoon Mr Turner. Welcome to Welford Hall. Please drive to the front door where Mr and Mrs Hopkins are awaiting your arrival.'

The huge gates slowly began to open and Bryn obeyed his instructions to drive the two hundred yards to the house. Shan and the boys sat in silent awe of the tree lined drive and the magnificent house that came into view as they neared. As promised there were people at the front door smiling and waiting.

The Welsh contingency had arrived at around 4 pm and Isobel had an evening meal planned in the main dining room so that the families could get to know each other. William and Isabel welcomed the Turners at the main door as they arrived. Shan was nervous; she felt in awe of the opulence and splendour of the house. Isobel walked towards Shan as she stepped out of the car and kissed her cheek. Isabel had the grace of a lady and the warmth of a loving mother.

'I am so pleased to meet you, Shan; it's wonderful that we can have the rest of today with you before the wedding tomorrow.'

Isabel greeted the gentlemen then put her arm into Shan's and guided her into the house. Their bags were taken to their rooms; Isabel and William took Bryn and Shan through the house and into the back garden where tea was waiting on the lawn. The boys were too excited to drink tea and went for a stroll around the grounds.

The weather forecast for the weekend of the wedding was good and the house and gardens had never looked better. No-one would ever call William careful with his money but it was fair to say he was glad he only had the one daughter to marry off.

As the four sat drinking their tea you couldn't miss the Marquee straight ahead of them. It was enormous. When Isabel noticed Shan looking at it she commented.

'I think it may be a little on the big side but if the weather turns nasty we may have to have the ceremony under cover. You know what our weather is like Shan, totally unpredictable, no matter what they say on television.' she laughed.

'My wife thinks of everything, Bryn,' William winked.

'It's wonderful Isabel; I can't wait to see everything.'

'And of course you shall, but for now I will show you your room. Call the boys, William.'

Their rooms were on the second floor. The boys shared a large twin suite with views over the rear garden. Bryn and Shan had an even bigger suite and the en suite bathroom was something Shan could only dream of. It had a Jacuzzi bath big enough for two, twin basins, a huge shower and it was all set in Italian marble with under floor heating. Shan hadn't needed to bring her own toiletries. There were brands she had never heard of and looked very expensive.

'Don't get any ideas Bryn,' Shan said as she watched Bryn testing out the comfort level of the large bed by bouncing on it. She had a wicked smile.

Shan unpacked their bags and hung her outfit for the wedding carefully so that the few creases would fall out.

'Look at these curtains Bryn, they are so thick and heavy,' Shan stroked them as she looked out of the window that those beautiful drapes dressed.

Their room overlooked the front garden and from the bedroom you could appreciate the lovely flower beds and long tree lined drive to the main front gate.

The bed was big with far too many pillows and scatter cushions. The furniture was old but in perfect condition, perhaps classical and stylish is a better description.

'I'm glad I don't have to clean this house,' Shan mumbled as she unpacked her underwear, wondering which one of the many drawers to put them in.

'I think I'll have a nap before dinner, love. It's been a long drive.' Bryn stretched his arms and yawned.

'Okay, cariad. I'll have a bath in the swimming pool,' she laughed as she watched her husband's eyelids close.

By the time they went down for dinner Alex and Susannah had arrived and there were kisses all round. Alex was always pleased to be with his brothers and they chatted all evening. William Hopkins Jnr. seemed to enjoy the company of the boys and they all got on well together.

Isobel was a great host and managed the service of an excellent dinner. It seemed that the staff could read her mind as with only a look they knew what was expected of them.

Shan's early apprehensions were forgotten. Isabel and William were genuinely nice people. Not at all what Shan thought they would be like when considering their wealth.

The dinner was superb; Beef Wellington at its best and far too much. William had brought his best claret from the cellar which was left to breath on the sideboard, but not for too long. A wonderful evening which Bryn and Shan will remember for years to come.

After dinner they all enjoyed an hour in what they called the 'William Room'. Isobel explained that through the years since the house had been in the Hopkins family, that room had been used for the men only, where they would retire after dinner to enjoy a brandy and cigar. The ladies would have their own room in a different part of the house and amuse themselves.

'A very old fashioned idea. Don't you agree Shan?' Isobel pontificated with a smile.

Shan obediently concurred with a nod.

'When William and I took over the house I had it redecorated to get rid of that dreadful smell of cigars and found that it made a cosy room for everyone to enjoy together after dinner.'

'And rightly so my dear and so very modern too,' agreed William with a smile and a knowing look to Bryn who had no idea what they were talking about but responded with a smile anyway.

There were a few cognacs taken in the 'William Room' that night with the excuse of toasting the couple on the eve of their wedding. It was a joining of the two families and happiness was firmly on the agenda.

Back in their bedroom, exhausted, Bryn and Shan undressed for bed.

'I love our farm Bryn but this is something else; not a muddy puddle or sheep in sight.'

Shan smiled as she slipped into bed with her husband of thirty five years.

'Tomorrow will be just wonderful.'

And it was. It was even better than wonderful. The day started early for the family and was a little overcast. The mother of the bride and the mother of the groom were up before everyone and chatted together over coffee; reminiscing over their children's childhood and telling tales neither child would appreciate being aired. As they sat around the kitchen table together, they each silently recognised how different their lives were, yet how much of a bond they shared with the union of their children. They considered their children lucky to have such mothers and laughed together, imagining what Alex and Susannah would think if they could hear their conversation. Nearly an hour passed and the sun was beginning to wake, which spurred the ladies into action. They walked into the garden arm in arm.

The Marquee was unbelievable. Everything was white.

'What do you think of the white roses Shan? William says they're too much.'

'No, no Isabel! Everything is perfect. I don't know how you've done it all.'

'Well I had some help; but to be honest I quite enjoy organising this sort of thing.'

Shan couldn't believe that there were even crystal chandeliers in the Marquee.

William's voice bellowed from the house. 'The hair people are here darling.'

'Come on, Shan, we're in for a treat. Have you heard of Harding & Buckley from the West End?' She didn't wait for a reply. 'Well I've asked them to send a few of their people to make us glamorous. They've got their work cut out Shan.' Isabel laughed as she took Shan's arm and led her back indoors.

They went upstairs to Isabel's bedroom where Susannah was coming out of the bathroom and about to be tended by the beauticians and hairdressers in attendance. The bedroom was more like an apartment and Susannah was under strict instructions from her mother not to leave the room in case she bumped into the groom who had the freedom of the house. Shan thought her bedroom was big but this one was enormous. Isobel thought it would be fun for all the ladies to get ready together and it would make it easier for the hairstylists and beauticians to have all their equipment in one place.

'Take this robe, Shan. You'll find everything you need in the bathroom. They can start on me after Susannah, so there's no rush.'

Time passed quickly and after their pampering the ladies looked quite exquisite. With perfect makeup and beautifully styled hair they donned the wedding attire. Isobel and Shan presented themselves at the front door with their husbands to welcome the guests.

Isabel left the serving of drinks and the wedding breakfast feast to her staff on the day. They had all been working for her for many years and she trusted them totally to follow the plans they had drawn up together. So that the staff could enjoy themselves in the evening Isabel had booked serving staff from an agency to take over at around 6 pm The food for the evening buffet had been pre-cooked by her own staff so drinks would be served with a cold buffet around eight o'clock; there could be no mistakes.

The sun arrived and was bright in a cloudless sky, no more than you would expect from a party hosted by the Hopkins' family. Time passed so quickly and the guests had nearly all arrived. They were given a glass of champagne on arrival and then shown to their seats in the garden by an elderly gentleman who had supervised the upkeep of the gardens for many years. John was well past retirement but William asked him, as a special favour, if he could help them out on the day of the wedding. He was dressed in black tie and had the biggest smile as he slowly led each guest to their chair.

Alex had decided to have groomsmen rather than the traditional best man. That way he could include both brothers and it also meant that Susannah's brother, William, could be included.

Shan was so proud of her boys she patted the tears from her cheeks trying to protect her beautiful makeup. As she and Bryn took their seats, they enjoyed the scent of the roses and the thousands of petals scattered on a pathway down the centre aisle to the awaiting groom and his men.

The guest chatted until the proceedings commenced. The bridal march was played by a string quartet and Susannah began her walk, on her father's arm, down the aisle to Alex who was waiting for his bride. The guests turned to look at her as she walked, she was so beautiful, so confident, a vision of loveliness. Alex held out his hand as she neared. His Mam was convinced he had a tear in his eye.

Bryn took his wife's hand in his as their boy and his bride walked back up the aisle as Mr and Mrs Alex Turner.

106

What a magnificent couple they were. The photographer took over an hour to complete his part and the guests were then invited to go into the marquee where Alex and Susannah waited to welcome them under an arch of white roses at the entrance.

A sumptuous meal was served with wine unlimited then after the extremely long speeches, musical entertainment from a full band played a varied selection of new and old tunes. The music could be heard for miles in the still of a beautiful summer's day as the wedding breakfast meandered tactfully into the evening celebrations and over one hundred more guests arrived. The festivities ended before midnight and all were asleep soon after.

After a light breakfast served in the garden the following day, Bryn, Shan and the boys packed their belongings and left around noon. It was a smooth exit with loving farewells and promises to return. Alex and Susannah had an overnight flight to Jamaica to pick up a cruise ship for two blissful weeks travelling around the Caribbean, compliments of William and Isobel, of course.

James and Edward chatted all the way home in the back seat of the car. Bryn and Shan travelled in silence both thinking about the excitement of their time spent with William and Isobel; their beautiful home and the opulent wedding day they had given their son and his bride. After a long journey the car turned up the lane to the farm, seemingly knowing its own way. Indoors, Shan put the kettle on as Bryn carried the bags up to their bedroom. The boys changed and went to check on the animals; a neighbour across the valley had been looking after the farm whilst they were away and they had a boy in each day to feed the animals that weren't grazing.

Sitting in their old but comfy armchairs the couple enjoyed a nice cup of strong tea.

'Give me a cuppa over that posh champagne any day,' Bryn was back in his comfort zone.

'Oh, I dunno love; I could get used to it.' Shan teased.

There was no response from Bryn, and Shan knew when to leave well alone.

'Did we make the right decision Shan? You know about the farm I mean. Should we have sold it when Dad died?'

'What you on about now, love?'

'Well, we could have 'ad some money and bought a nice house. We could have gone to England even, by the sea.'

'And what's wrong with Wales and the lovely beaches we have here Bryn? Don't you talk so daft, we have everything we want and you have to think of the boy's livelihood too.' The matter was dropped by both but they had experienced such a different way of life that weekend. They'd had a taste of the good life and it unsettled them, even Shan; although she would never admit that to Bryn.

Bryn drove James and Edward into town that night for a few beers with their friends.

'I don't know where you two get your energy from,' Bryn was beginning to feel his age; he had worked hard over the years. 'Don't go phoning me to pick you youngsters up late tonight; I'll be tucked up in bed by 10 o'clock.' He slipped James a ten pound note for a taxi home.

Bryn drove back to the farm with a smile of pride on his face. The boys had turned out well. James and Edward following in the family tradition of farming and Alex, the clever one, working in London, the first Turner to be a solicitor. Wouldn't any Dad be proud?

Shan and Bryn watched a film before going to bed early that night. They didn't even hear the boys come in.

Alex and Susannah enjoyed a wonderful Caribbean cruise. Their last port of call was Barbados where they took a taxi to Carlisle Bay and spent the day at the famous 'Boat Yard.' Of course it wasn't actually a boat yard but may have been before tourism took over. It had a jetty dipping into the turquoise sea and huge floats for the more energetic to have fun with. The Barbadian food in the restaurant, which looked like an extended shack, was out of this world. The cocktails were lethal and the loud music made it impossible to have a conversation. They promised each other that they would come back soon.

It could have been the effect of the cocktails but Alex got a little serious as they enjoyed their last hour on their sun beds before the taxi ride back to the ship.

'I've been thinking darling.'

'Oh dear, that's a bit scary,' Susannah teased.

'No, serious love, about our future.'

Susannah was taken aback and sat up to face Alex.

'What d'you mean, our future, Alex?'

Alex sat up and took Susannah's hand in his.

'I love you so much, darling, and I want you to be happy; I really do.'

'And?' Susannah was getting concerned about this conversation it seemed to be leading somewhere.

'Please hear me out. Could you imagine yourself living in the country?' he put a finger to her lips before she could speak.

'Think about the life we could have. It would be quiet, so different from the hectic pace we have now in the city. There'd be more time for each other. We wouldn't have to move far and we could commute each day. A nice country house with land. Eventually I could start up a business of breeding dogs.' Alex stopped talking to allow his words to sink in. It was surely out of the blue and he didn't want to throw all his ideas at Susannah at once.

Susannah couldn't contain herself any longer. Her eyes grew wide and she stammered her response.

'And where has all this come from Alex? We are solicitors, that's what we have trained to do and we earn a lot of money doing it. I love my job and I'm dammed good at it. We should be living where our jobs are not commuting, as you say. I have to be near the office, my job is not nine to five as a criminal lawyer. You know how often I am called to the police station in the middle of the night to sort out problems when our clients get arrested at all hours. Alex, I have to be there?'

'I know that and we'll make sure you're not too far away.'

'Why has everything changed Alex? You chose your profession?'

'My work as a conveyancing lawyer is really not that exciting love.'

'But dogs Alex, I didn't even know you had that much of an interest in dogs.'

'It's probably the farmer in me. I love all animals but I think I could earn a good living eventually. It may take a few years to get started but if we live in commuting distance we'll still have a good income. Maybe one day you'll want to settle down and we can start our own family, where better than working and living in our own paradise, in the country?'

Susannah was quiet. Most unusual. Alex grew hopeful, at least she was thinking about it. He had expected objections at the very least; even an almighty row.

Susannah chose her words carefully, just like the good solicitor she had become.

'I know you haven't been truly content in London and with work recently, but I thought that if I didn't bring the subject up it would go away. I could see how happy you were when we went to Llandrindod Wells to visit your parents. The fact that I love my work so much has made me selfish and I want you to be happy, my love.'

Alex was amazed and his face showed it.

'I don't regret the path I've taken Su. I would never have met you if I'd stayed at home but I want the best of both worlds and if I work hard I know we can have everything. You are my reason for living and I promise I'll make you the happiest woman on this planet.'

Alex stood up and felt his feet burn on the hot sand. He pulled Susannah up and kissed her passionately, caring not of the spectators enjoying the display.

Soon he released that Susannah had one stipulation on which there was to be no compromise.

'I want to keep the London apartment Alex; I need to be there sometimes during the week. You can have your fancy home in the country but not at the expense of losing my apartment. I realise that this will slow things down as far as buying that second property and we will be apart sometimes during the week but that is my condition and I will not move on it. Of course I'll have to get Philip to agree to an 'on call' rota so that, at least, I will know when I'll be at home with you or at the apartment. I'm sure Phil and I can come to an agreement, of sorts.' Susannah laughed at the thought of bargaining with the boss. 'Yes, I think it could even work out for the best.'

Alex was surprised with Susannah's calm acceptance so Alex continued with more news; the best was yet to come.

'I've been talking to James and Ed and although it was agreed that my education was to replace my share of the farm, there are prospects that have changed things and they want to give me some cash which we can use as a deposit for a house; what do you think about looking when we get home?'

'You seemed to have everything worked out, my scheming little husband.' Susannah quite liked this unforeseen determination in her new husband.

James and Edward had been discussing the prospects of the farm with Alex as a long term project when they were together at the wedding. It seemed that things would need to change to support the boys and possibly future families for them both and a comfortable retirement for their parents. A developer had been pestering Bryn for many years in the hope that he would sell a strip of land near the main road for housing. Bryn was of the old school and would sacrifice everything to keep his farm in tact but the boys knew it was the only way to survive and inject a little cash into the future of their business. Bryn had finally seen reason and conceded. They would be able to give Alex a portion to help him set up his own business.

The boys were very generous to Alex in making such a decision. Bryn had always said that Alex had his share of the farm through the fees of his University education, which cost Bryn a small fortune and took every penny of his savings. This unexpected windfall would make such a difference to Alex's dream of a place in the country.

The cruise had been the perfect holiday for Alex and Susannah and they took many, many photos to show the family. They returned home exhausted even though the only thing they did was enjoy themselves on board the cruise liner and the islands they visited. A perfect wedding, a perfect honeymoon and a perfect life to come.

It seems that after such perfection the only thing ahead would have to be a perfect life. If only life were written in a book and you could read the last chapter to find out how everything ends. Alex and Susannah could never have imagined how extraordinary their life would become.

Death and broken hearts.

Chapter 18

Alex and Susannah Begin Life as Man and Wife.

Alex and Susannah arrived home safely from their honeymoon cruise; refreshed, relaxed and ready to start their life as man and wife. The first thing Susannah did was ring her parents. Excitedly she told her mother all about the adventure and the wonderful beaches in the Caribbean. That seemed to take forever then she broke the news about their idea to buy a home in the country with a plan to breed dogs.

Alex could hear the reaction clearly.

'What on earth do you know about dogs Susannah?'

'Mum! Listen! It's Alex's dream to have a place in the country and I can commute so my job will be exactly the same.'

Even though Susannah seemed to be positive, Alex was still a little surprised by her mother's reaction.

'Don't worry about mum and dad love, I can sort them out.'

They had an early night it was always a good remedy for any problems they might have.

It didn't take long to get back into the old routine at work but of course things had changed; they were now Mr and Mrs Turner. Lunchtime on that first day back Susannah went into Alex's office to speak with him.

'Think about what I'm saying Alex, don't jump in until I've had my say. The thing is I intend to keep my maiden name of Susannah Hopkins for work purposes. It makes sense; I have built my reputation on that name. I'm known by everyone as Susannah Hopkins and the Firm want me to keep it that way.' She smiled and waited.

'If that's what you want I can't do much about it but I'm not happy love. It's only for work though?'

'Absolutely! Just for work.' Susannah breathed a sigh of relief; she had thought there would be more in the way of objections. Things were looking up or maybe they were still in honeymoon mode and loved up, as the youngsters say.

Alex outwardly accepted the situation and put it to the back of his mind for the time being. He was excited about the thought of moving to the country and wasted no time in getting appointments to view properties within a certain radius of London. He had his share of the cash from the sale of part of the farm and now, didn't need to sell the London apartment. All together he had three properties lined up to view the next weekend, all in Hertfordshire. He broke the news to Susannah.

On Saturday they drove north and viewed the first two houses. The properties were both quite remote, no neighbours within a mile. The first was very old and needed major construction work to make it habitable. It had three large bedrooms. The downstairs was adequate and there were several acres of land with out buildings suitable for renovation which would make ideal kennels. Alex could see that Susannah didn't like it and agreed that there was too much work for him to take on and it was miles from a railway station which was an essential ingredient in their plan to commute. The second was very similar to the first and the couple decided to take a break and reconsider what they had seen.

They stopped for lunch at a quiet country pub and discussed the two properties. Neither of them were impressed enough with the first two and recapped on their findings before striking them from the list.

'I hope the next house is better Alex or the whole day will be wasted.'

'Oh I don't know love, it's nice having a day out together and not worry about work for a change.'

Susannah reached across the table and took her husbands hand in hers. She loved his strong chin and dark brown eyes but most of all his Welsh charm, if there was such a thing then Alex had it. She smiled.

Alex had purposely kept the next house until last. On paper it had exactly what he was looking for, but he was still a little apprehensive.

It was a cottage on the outskirts of a small village with a four acre back and side garden. The conversation Alex had with the Estate Agent when he arranged the viewing appointment seemed to imply that it was a well known village.

'You must have heard of Camberley Edge' he enthused 'famous for the annual flower festival.' The agent expected at least a little recognition; he was disappointed.

Alex had seen pictures of the layout of the property and garden. Although in a village it was on the outskirts and far enough away to consider building kennels without causing noise and disruption to neighbours.

After their pub lunch the couple returned to the car. Alex put the post code of the house into his sat-nav and off they went. It didn't take long to reach Camberley Edge and driving through the village they were more than a little impressed. It was quaint and well kept. Every property was different as if they had all been built at different times, extending the village year by year. They noticed the lovely gardens as they drove through the High Street passing the church, the school and the pub. There were a few shops and a post office with tables and chairs outside. 'Well! What do you think love?' Alex was hoping for more enthusiasm this time.

'Not bad, not bad at all.' Alex was content with that response.

They found the house easily and the couple were delighted with what they saw. As they got out of the car in front of 'Jasmine Cottage' Susannah breathed in the sweet scent of the Jasmine which filled the garden and draped the front door. A little over grown but beautiful all the same.

Inside the cottage the rooms were dated as far as decoration was concerned. They had been told that an elderly couple had spent all their married life in the cottage and didn't really change it at all so they knew there was work to be done; but only cosmetic as they say in the trade.

The rooms were bigger than usual for a cottage, both downstairs and up. Upstairs there were three large bedrooms and a bathroom, no en-suite but there was room for one to be added

115

and possibly a walk in closet for Susannah's clothes. They may have to lose a bedroom to fit it all in but they could manage with two bedrooms for now and, maybe extend the property later.

Alex was eager to check out the land at the back, he wasn't disappointed in what he saw.

'Call this a garden? It's almost as big as the sheep's field in Lland'od.' He was delighted. It was far better than he expected. There were a few out buildings but Alex had a 'plan'. Knock them down and rebuild. Simple!

'It's perfect Alex, a blank canvas that we can make our own. Before we alter it in any way though I'd like to live in it for a while. You know, get a feel for the place.' His wife's comments were positive; she liked it. What more could he ask?

'Any thing you want babe.' He felt as if he would burst with joy.

In work on the following Monday morning they told everyone the good news. Over the weekend they had decided that Alex would quit his job as soon as possible and start work on the out buildings, the sooner they were in place the sooner they could earn some money from it. After buying the house there was enough left over for the building work if Alex did some himself.

He spoke to Mr. Benjamin; a month was the total amount of notice he would have to work.

'We'll be sorry to lose you Alex; you've been an asset to the firm.'

Alex was grateful for his kind words but all he could think of was his new project.

In less than two months they had moved into the house and Alex immediately started searching for a few good dog breeders where he could buy his dogs and start the breeding line. Four bitches that would parent the dogs they needed. A Golden Labrador Retriever, a Black Labrador, a Cocker and Springer Spaniels.

Alex had a plan, more than just dog breeding. He wanted to make a name for himself in the world of gun dogs. He planned to breed the best; and train them. He wanted to manage shoots for interested people far and wide. He had a mission and there was no stopping him now.

The dogs he chose to start this dream were the best he could fined. Excellent examples of Labradors and Spaniels, perhaps even show level but definitely from a good strain of working gun dogs. Alex decided to start breeding as soon as he could and sell the pups advertising them as good family pets. The first batch would live in the house until they were old enough to be found homes. The sooner the better, they would make money to continue the plans he had for training other dogs to work. To breed dogs you had to be licensed and Alex would eventually need to custom-build kennels and work sheds that were to be the best, nothing less for Alex's dogs. Puppies needed care and attention, heat lamps and plenty of indoor space for them to run and exercise, this alone would be expensive. The pups that were to be sold ready for work would have to be kept for around eight months in order to be trained effectively; they had to be of a certain standard.

Labrador Retrievers are renowned for their fearless determination on the command of their master. Throwing themselves into lakes and swimming to retrieve the target, often struggling with a large bird in their mouth and proudly presenting it at the master's feet.

Spaniels, on the other hand, were the experts at flushing out the prey from cover. Their temperament is energetic and jumpy. They can usually be seen at the beating line getting the birds into the target space, cleverly keeping close in crops and woods.

The whole procedure is a joint enterprise and the dogs love every minute of it.

The work of upgrading the house would have to wait and Susannah was happy with that. She wasn't in favour of keeping the pups in the house long term so, to keep his wife happy, he had to complete the work as soon as he possibly could. The old out buildings had been demolished so finishing the new ones would make his dream come true. For the time being the four dogs would sleep in a lean-to on the side of the house. It was dry and not too cold.

At first Susannah tried to be home most evenings and every weekend giving reasons at work as settling in time. Things soon changed, she felt it was too much to go home every single evening and started staying over at the London apartment more often, taking her share of out of hours calls from the police and their clients. Alex understood her position and how she felt; in fact he was quietly pleased to be able to work later into the evenings and drop into bed exhausted. When she did come home he always made a special effort by having a hot meal ready and her favourite merlot open and breathing.

After an especially long, hard day at work on the main building Alex was exhausted, but thought he'd ring his wife to say goodnight. It was around 10 p.m. and he was expecting Susannah to be in bed either reading the papers for court the following day or maybe watching a film on T.V. When she answered she seemed irritated.

'What, Alex? I'm in the pub.'

'Okay love, just wanted to say goodnight,' he was disappointed. 'Oh! Will you be home tomorrow evening? I'll cook something special.'

'I'll let you know. Goodnight.'

The line went dead and Alex held the phone in his hand for a while, a little shocked.

The noise in the pub came over loud and clear; so did Phil's voice in the background. Should he be worried? He thought about his wife drinking and enjoying herself without him. The green-eyed monster reared its ugly head.

'No,' he said out loud 'not my Susannah she loves me.' He fell asleep but with a heavy heart.

There were many nights when Susannah didn't come home. Alex put them to the back of his mind and threw himself into his own work. It had been decided that the house decorating would be put on hold until the kennels and other out- houses were finished. It wasn't great having the four dogs in the lean-to, especially when it was raining and they had been out for a walk it would have a scent all of its own which sometimes filtered through the house. On Susannah's away nights he'd let them come into the lounge with him but she always knew. Their long hair and damp smell would confirm the deceit, which caused arguments between the couple.

It was a difficult time. They both worked extremely hard and sometimes didn't appreciate each others efforts. On their evenings together there was often tension. Alex would ply his beautiful wife with her favourite wine and they would relax a little knowing things would get easier. It wouldn't be this hard for ever surely?

Chapter 19

2016 - Louise's Prison Visitor.

'What the………… I'll never get used to that bloody bell.' Tracy needed to be woken up gently in the mornings but Lockwood Park Prison officers thought differently. Louise got up as soon as the door was unlocked and went out onto the landing to get away from Tracy, her foul language and morning cigarette. Amanda was out too.

'Let's go get our breakfast Louise; I'm famished.' Amanda was always hungry.

'Tracy is getting worse every day.' Louise made conversation.

'She's one tough lady; don't think of crossing her, Louise.'

'I know,' Louise touched Amanda's arm in thanks.

'Anderson!' Louise turned to face the officer calling her. She would never get used to being called by her surname.

'Your father has contacted the prison, Anderson; he wants to see you.' The plump officer growled. The same officer that had escorted her to the funeral.

Louise was surprised but tried not to show her feelings. Weakness is not a healthy emotion to show these people, even the screws.

'Yes, Okay.' she said quickly. 'When?'

'Next Saturday.' The officer was matter of fact with the information.

Louise could feel her heart beating fast and was getting light headed at the thought of seeing her father after all this time, what could he want? As the realisation was sinking in a smile grew on her face. Her thoughts flashed from one to another. Maybe he and Abigail Flint had parted at last and he wanted to make amends. The smile disappeared and thoughts of her mother and the funeral came flooding back. She had time; maybe she would refuse to see him.

'I didn't know you had a father Louise. You never mentioned him,' said Amanda.

'He left us for the 'Tart,' she smiled. 'But that was a lifetime ago. Should I see him, Amanda? What do you think?'

'Family is family, love. Give him a chance.'

Louise made the decision to see her dad and began looking forward to Saturday. Feelings of disloyalty to her mother were always at the back of her mind but she needed someone and there was only her dad left. She secretly hoped that Abigail had dumped him and he was coming to say he was sorry for what he had done to her and mum. Mostly she was confused, and common sense told her to wait rather than speculate.

Saturday arrived. After lunch she was taken to the visiting hall. A luminous sash was placed around her upper body for identification in the hall. Louise had never had a visitor before and she was anxious not knowing what to expect. It was new and exciting.

As Louise walked into the hall she was surprised to see just how big it was. The windows were high and barred, as you would expect. The ceilings were higher than double the height of other rooms and gave the hall a feeing of light and airiness. There were dozens of tables with chairs either side. Surprisingly there was an area in one corner set up for children to play. It had lots of toys, books and plastic tables and chairs. Louise was happy to see a machine where you can buy tea, coffee or hot chocolate; that would be a pleasant treat. Then she spotted another vending machine with chocolate and crisps. Quite a party she thought.

Louise sat with all the other expectant inmates, in silence. All impatiently watching the large white door leading to the reception area and the world outside.

It wasn't long before the visitors appeared, filing in through the doorway. It seemed like forever. Then, she saw her dad. He looked lost as he scanned the room for her. She put up her hand to help him and his face lit up as he walked towards her. She noticed he was thinner and his hair whiter. Unexpected emotion overcame her and she stood up to greet him, both tearful as they hugged, neither one wanting to let go.

Words were difficult but George started the conversation as they sat down opposite each other, across the table.

'I didn't know a thing until the letter, darling. I would have been there for you had I known.' Their hands grasped each others across the table as he spoke.

'I never stopped loving you Lou, never for one moment.'

'What letter dad?'

'Madge, in the Post Office tracked me down. Don't ask me how? She said she had been trying to get hold of me from the start but it was harder than she thought. After that I had a big problem trying to get a visiting order to see you. Apparently I should be on your list but they said you don't have one. Well. All that doesn't matter now. I'm here.' He smiled and squeezed her hand.

'Where are you living, dad?'

'Abi and I have a flat in the Midlands.'

'Abi? You're still with her then?'

George was disappointed that Louise was still bitter about all that had happened but he was determined to move forward and take Louise with him.

'Yes darling, but I'm here for you today.'

'Sorry dad, thanks.' Louise squeezed his hand. Her dad was back in her life and that was so important to her.

'Now sweetheart, tell me everything, right from the start.'

Louise wasn't comfortable talking about her lover to her dad but he had to know everything.

'We had to move out of the vicarage after you left, so mum and I rented a cottage just off the High Street. It was actually up for sale but the owner knew mum and was happy to rent it until he got a buyer. Although mum never actually said anything I knew she was grateful that you sent that divorce settlement cheque to Madge for us. We put the whole lot down as a deposit on our cottage leaving a small mortgage. Where did you get the money from dad?'

'It was some savings that Abi and I had for a deposit on a house but we both decided you and mum needed it more. We rent our flat and probably will for a while.'

Louise continued. 'I expect you know from Madge that she gave mum a job at the post office. She also grew more orchids to sell, some quite rare so we had enough money to live well. It took mum two years to come to terms with what you did to us, dad, but she slowly got some of her bounce back.'

Louise smiled thinking of her dear mother.

'It must have been hard for you, love. I thought about contacting you all the time.'

'It wouldn't have worked dad. Mum never forgave you.'

'Anyway,' Louise went on 'Alex and Susannah bought old Mrs Crawshay's place, Jasmine Cottage. I got friendly with Alex; helping him with his dogs and stuff. He helped me with school work; I was studying 'A' level Law and he was a lawyer so it made sense. I helped him and he helped me. Susannah stayed in their London apartment quite a lot, so Alex and I were company for each other. I know it was wrong dad, but we were special together. At least, he was special to me. I know now it was one way, but I believed we had a future together and he let me think that.'

The whole story poured out. Everything that had happened. Alex's dreams and ambitions. The way he worked so hard with his dogs and building his dream of dog breeding and training. Susannah's life in London. There was so much to take in but George listened carefully.

George squeezed her hand gently, 'Go on, love.'

'Mum didn't know anything about it only that he was kind to me and we were friends. He told me he loved me and I was his life, his future. It must have been all lies.'

Louise looked down at her hands as she continued. 'I didn't like seeing them together. I was walking along the High Street after school one afternoon and saw them talking to mum. As I got nearer I heard Alex tell mum that Susannah was pregnant but she wasn't to tell a soul. Before mum could respond she saw me walking towards them. Alex turned around;

he looked shocked to see me so close. I mumbled some excuse and walked quickly past. I wanted to hide from the world; he had betrayed me with this woman. A baby! I couldn't believe it. When I knew Susannah was back in London I went to Jasmine Cottage to confront Alex. He seemed shocked that I was so upset. There was an almighty row and I threatened to tell Susannah all about us. He was so angry.'

Louise paused. George could see her pain and he felt such anger towards the man that had treated her so badly and had broken his little girl's heart.

Louise whispered the words that George needed to hear. 'I didn't kill him dad, I really didn't kill Alex. I loved him.' Louise bowed her head and wept pitifully. Father and daughter held hands in silence.

'Why didn't mum go to court and speak up for you?'

'My lawyer said she would be an unreliable witness because she was on the verge of a breakdown and didn't really understand what was happening. The pills that the doctor gave her made her sleep most of the time. He said that it was the alternative to hospital. In her state of stupor she would tell people it was all her fault. Madge took care of her.'

'Well! If you didn't kill him then who did?'

'You believe me?'

'Of course I do darling. You're my little girl.'

The bell rang loudly and the guards who had been sitting around the hall got up to usher the visitors out quickly.

Louise clung to George.

'Don't you worry about a thing darling. I'll get you out of here. I promise.'

Louise trembled as she watched him leave.

George left HMP Lockwood Park with so much left unsaid. He hadn't previously given any thought to the fact that Louise might be innocent. He was ashamed to admit that after hearing Madge's version it had seemed she did it. The fact she believed Susannah was staying in London that night and Alex would be alone made it look premeditated and because she had been in the house so many times she knew where everything was kept including his guns. He knew he had a lot of work to do.

It took George hours to get back to the flat and Abigail. They had chosen to move to the Midlands for two reasons; it meant that no-one would know them and also it was a good place to find work in a factory for himself and in a shop for Abigail. George got a job in the well known Nuts & Bolts factory and Abigail worked in a popular high street fashion outlet. They were happy together for the most part. Although there were times, as you would expect, when George felt sadness that he had caused Daphne and Louise such pain. Abigail was his rock and saw him through those bad times with love and tenderness.

The anguish and devastation they knew that they had caused to Daphne and Louise weighed heavily on their conscience. They chose to give all the money they had to Daphne knowing she needed to find a home for her and Louise. This left George penniless but he could work and build a new life for them both.

Abigail listened to the drama of George's day.

'If Louise didn't kill Alex, then who did, George?' Abigail wanted to believe Louise hadn't committed murder but it seemed to her that she had.

'I don't know Abi. I have to find out who had most to gain, a motive.'

They both racked their brains for an alternative. Something solid to overturn the jury's conviction. Evidence that would exonerate Louise. Abigail thought for a while and came up with the only thing she could think of.

'There's only one person George. His wife; what's her name?'

'Susannah. I've thought about that all the way home.'

George was emotionally and physically exhausted. The couple decided they would eat their supper and go to bed early to sleep on the thoughts mulling around in their heads and start again tomorrow. The delicious smell coming from the oven reassured him. He was home.

After dinner the pair sat together on the sofa, the desire for sleep still with them, but the conversation drifted back to Susannah.

Abigail couldn't help herself; she really believed she had something.

'Perhaps she knew about Louise and wasn't in London that night. Perhaps she was watching the house or, with her money, she may have had someone do the job for her.'

'We're not in America now Abi.' George smiled. 'Having said that, Sherlock, you have a good point.'

After a night of tossing and turning George got up at 6 a.m. and started to write things down. He used that process when writing his sermons for the Sunday Church services in Camberley Edge. He loved that time of his life but things were not what they seemed with Daphne. He had loved her for years but there was always something missing. Something he had found with Abigail. He told Daphne he'd tried to fight the attraction and she laughed at his weakness. There were never any more discussions between the married couple after he left home. Yes, he had secretly prepared for his exit and he knew it would be painful for all concerned but would it have been better to stay and be unhappy?

Words flowed onto the paper before him. Reasons for whom he suspected; there was really only one clear candidate at this point but he tried to be open minded. The whys and wherefores of how the deed could have been carried out. Was Susannah in the house before Alex came in from working in the garden? Maybe she had heard Louise confront Alex and realised that she could use Louise as a scapegoat; Susannah had said she was staying in London. But did she?

The task ahead was great but he had to start somewhere and he believed London would be the best place. By the time Abigail got up he had decided to go to London on Monday. They rang each others place of employment to say that there was a tummy bug going around and they were taking a day to recover and avoid spreading their germs to colleagues. They both sounded convincing. George, especially, had learned the technique of lying to a good level, but he wasn't proud of himself.

He rang Madge to find out if she knew the name of the firm of solicitors that Susannah worked for.

'Yes George, I do. I had the odd conversations with Susannah and she once mentioned Philip Scott as being one of the partners of four in their firm. Does that help?'

'It certainly does, Madge. I'll find him somehow.'

George promised to ring Madge later and explain what was happening. But for now he wanted to get down to London and make waves.

They were in the car by 10 am and on their way to the big city. George put the address of the firm into his sat-nav and they were there in no time.

George had always had a presence about him which probably came from his theological training. He walked into the reception area and asked to speak with Mrs Susannah Turner.

'You mean, Miss Hopkins?' The receptionist corrected George, then said she was in court and didn't know what time she'd be back.

'I'll wait' said George with a look that said 'don't argue with me'.

After the couple sat in reception for about half an hour in came a tall, striking gentleman carrying too many files. He put them on the desk quickly as they began to slide from his grip, complaining about the need for so many files for one court case. He spoke quietly with the receptionist and turned to George.

'Can I help you sir? Do you need to speak to a criminal lawyer?'

'No' said George firmly 'I need to speak to Susannah Turner.'

'Oh! You mean Susannah Hopkins; she uses her family name for work.'

'So I've been told. What time will she be back? It's personal.'

'She's just behind me. Probably in the building and probably powdering her nose, knowing Su.' Philip chuckled but George remaining stoic.

Then, in she walked. Not what George expected of a lawyer; more of a model.

Philip stopped her from dashing straight into her office 'Someone to see you Su, personal stuff.' He turned to George 'I didn't catch your name.'

George ignored him and walked towards Susannah.

'I need to talk to you about my daughter, Louise. Here or somewhere else?'

'Come into my office Mr Anderson, or should I call you Reverend?' There was a hint of sarcasm in her voice.

'Mr Anderson will do, Miss Hopkins. That is what you like being called?' George was ready for action. Susannah wasn't pregnant so George asked about her child.

'She stays with my parents. I have to work you understand. I am a widow; but of course you know that, don't you?' She said raising her voice arrogantly.

'You have a beautiful house in the country you no longer need.' George tried to provoke her further.

'That's my business. What is it exactly you want with me?'

George took a step closer.

'I want to know how you were involved in your late husband's death.'

Susannah didn't respond but George could see her expression was changing. She wondered how much he knew.

'I want to know who the father of your child is. Is it really Alex's?'

'I want to know when your affair with the moron in reception started.' Finally, I want to know if you planned your husbands demise with the moron or was it something you did alone as a reaction to your husbands infidelity.'

Susannah paled as she sat in the chair. Although George had been speculating he could see by Susannah's reaction he was spot on.

'You see, Mrs Turner. You may be a high-flying lawyer but I'm fighting for my daughter's freedom.' George deliberately used her married name.

The professional came back at George, just when he thought he had her where he wanted her.

'Well Mr Anderson that is a lot of 'I want to knows' you have there. Don't you realise that your daughter was found guilty by a jury in Crown Court? And rightly so. There was more than enough evidence to convict her and absolutely nothing to implicate me.'

George was relentless.

'People like you think you're clever and above the law but believe me Mrs Turner my daughter will be freed. If there is justice in this world you'll take her place in that prison. She has me now and I will get to the truth. You can bet your last penny on that.'

George and Abigail left the office.

Phil went into Susannah's office to find out what happened only to find Susannah tearful.

'My God Su, who was that? What happened?'

'That was Louise's father. He knows about us, about our affair.'

'He can't, love, he's guessing, digging. He's looking for your reactions.'

'He said straight out I killed Alex. He's relentless Phil. I know he'll cause trouble.'

'He can shout as much as he likes Su. He has no evidence to support those accusations. He would need factual evidence to appeal and he won't get any.'

'Phil, we have Eva-Lucy to think about now; it's not just about us anymore.' Susannah was clearly worried.

George and Abigail drove straight home. Trying to make sense of what they had learned, if anything. The couple were tired but had to get home for work the next day. How George's life had changed these past few years. He looked at Abi and smiled.

George knew in his heart that Susannah had murdered her adulterous husband and after that meeting he was totally convinced. He also knew that knowing and proving were two different things. They needed help. Professional help.

Back at the flat Abigail put the kettle on while George began writing his notes. He wrote every word he had said to Susannah and every word she'd said to him. He needed to look for clues, mistakes that Susannah might have made in what she'd said under pressure. Abi put his cup of tea in front of him.

'Start again tomorrow, love. You're tired; it's been a busy day for us both.'

'I need help Abi, real help, from a professional. Perhaps I can get some overtime at the factory. A private investigator won't come cheap.'

Abigail thought for a second then declared 'I've got some money put by. Since we gave Daphne all our money I've been saving hard towards a deposit for a house. I think we need to use that. We can save again later.'

George looked tenderly at Abigail and whispered.

'Thanks love.'

Chapter 20

George's Plan to Free Louise.

George Anderson knew he was the last and only hope for his only child, Louise, and was determined not to let his daughter down again. Such a great burden to bear yet he was, without a doubt, the man for the job. He had prayed every night for forgiveness for his sins since his betrayal. The day he'd walked out on Daphne and Louise haunted him but he accepted the heartache as his God given punishment, whatever that may be.

His prayers now were for guidance. He needed to find a way to get Louise out of prison and give her a life once more. But there were doubts; so many doubts and questions. Where do you start looking for a private investigator? How much do they cost? He even began to question his ability to fulfil his promise to Louise. Although he tried to remain positive all sorts of objections tumbled around in George's desperate thoughts.

He had to make a start and his computer seemed the best place. George wasn't as familiar with the internet as he would have liked and he wished he'd kept up with technology over the years. With Abigail's help he found what he was looking for and before he knew it he had an appointment that day with a private investigator not too far from home. George travelled to his appointment on his own. Abigail went to work.

The office was in a large office block not too far from the famous Bull Ring and one of the best shopping centres in that area. He parked the car in a nearby multi-storey car par and walked the short distance to meet the man that would be asked to solve all his problems. A little nervous, George walked into the foyer of the large building. There was no receptionist to ask so he looked around for directions. Opposite the lifts there was a wall with names, professions and where their offices were situated. Solicitors, Accountants, Financial Consultants and professions he'd never even heard, of like 'Reflexology'. Right there in the middle he found Alan P. James P.I. Floor 7 Room 736.

George headed for the lifts and found the office he was looking for. He knocked the door and within a second a man opened it. Alan Preston James was tall with black wavy hair and black rimmed glasses that framed his smiling eyes. The men shook hands and sat on leather chairs either side of the old wooden desk. George was impressed by what he saw. The office was neat and tidy without the musky smell he thought there would be. Alan was clean shaven and had on a smart suit and tie. The only thing George knew about private investigators was what he'd seen on television; always badly dressed and one even lived in a caravan. After fifty minutes George was content that every detail was discussed and noted. He handed over a copy of the file he had made with names, addresses and details that may or may not be of use to Alan James.

'Well I believe that's everything, Mr James. Now, can you help me?'

'It looks straightforward enough, Mr Anderson, and seems clear to me that this Susannah is quite a clever lady. A black widow with a careful aim.' He smiled. 'Now all I have to do is prove it and your girl walks free.'

Money was briefly mentioned; the first £500 was handed over for immediate expenses and the bill would come later.

George felt a sense of relief as he drove home to Abi. Penniless but happy. Mr James seemed to know what he was doing and George knew he needed a professional to sort out this mess. There was no alternative.

Alan Preston James certainly had the experience needed to do the job. The Metropolitan Police Service lost a good man the day Alan left. He had a degree in Criminal Psychology and had been a respected Criminal Profiler for many years. After leaving the Met. he worked freelance and travelled all over the world on high profile cases. Alan had never married but with his good looks and gentle manner he was never short of attractive young ladies.

It certainly wouldn't be a speedy process but George had faith in Alan James. He had to believe there was a chance; the alternative was too hard to contemplate.

When George arrived home Abi had his favourite meal waiting for him; baked cod with parsley sauce. The flat was small and they had rented it furnished, so it wasn't what either of them had been used to. Over the years time had been hard but it brought them closer together and they always looked forward. Their shabby little flat was fine for now but things would get better and they had each other, which meant the world to them both. George had never been so happy.

His conscience constantly reminded him of their beginning. It was as bad as you could ever imagine for a parish vicar and a girl young enough to be his daughter. An affair was not on George's agenda but he fell in love and knew it was the real thing. It was enough to give up everything for and he did. He loved Daphne in his own way but not like the love he felt for Abigail Flint. She had a reputation but, until George, no-one had taken the time to really get to know her. Abi was certainly not the hard core, loose woman that she presented herself as. Perhaps even George thought she was a bit rough around the edges at first but he soon recognised something more. In the sadness of losing her mother she showed vulnerability and let George into her psyche, her inner being. Maybe it had been, in fact, her innocence that allowed her to trust the boys who took advantage and boasted their results. Abi fell into a pattern of behaving as people expected; a tart.

After dinner, Abi busied herself with the washing up whilst George dozed on the sofa. Looking after him, even spoiling him a little was Abi's way of showing George how much she loved him and appreciated how much he gave up to be with her. He had dedicated his whole life to the ministry and his love for her took all that away. Joining George on the sofa after her chores were done, she leaned into his warm, safe body. Sleepily he put his arm around her shoulder pulling her close.

'I'm sorry to drag you into this mess, my love,' his voice broke as he spoke.

'I love you, George, whatever happens.'

The day had been difficult for George and no matter how hard he tried he couldn't get the picture of his little girl in a prison cell out of his mind. As he lay in bed that night thinking of what may be, tears filled his eyes and his heart ached.

'Thank you, God,' he silently prayed 'for this soft warm bed and the arms of a loving woman.' He slept until dawn.

Alan Preston James was up early and ready to put his plans into action. He had many friends in high, useful places and some who would know of William Hopkins, father of the black widow, as he called Susannah Turner. After a few telephone conversations he learned some interesting facts. It seems that Susannah and Philip Scott were known to all as an item and not just work colleagues, so George's random guess was spot on. Daddy had recently purchased an office in the City of London, something he had avoided in years. It was rumoured the firm of solicitors was to be called Hopkins, Hopkins and Scott. Alan had been given this information from an ex-colleague who disliked William Hopkins through dealings with him in the past and was happy to be able to help.

William Hopkins' friendship with Stephen Benjamin, the senior partner in Susannah's old firm, would make the transition easier. As usual there would undoubtedly be a transference of cash from one to another but William always got what he wanted and money was an easy sweetener.

Alan also discovered that Philip had moved into Susannah's apartment soon after Alex's demise, but still kept his own nearby. That appeared a little strange to Alan, why would Philip move in with Susannah whilst pregnant with another man's child? Why would he keep his apartment too? George had planted the seed of doubt that Susannah's baby was not Alex's and it looked that he could be right.

Another of Alan's 'friends in high places' was his next telephone call. Within the week he received a copy of the baby's birth certificate and guess who was down as the father? Philip Scott.

The picture was becoming clearer as each piece of information was uncovered. There was now a clear motive but Alan needed to get something more definite to take it to 'Appeal'. It would have to be filed. It was outside the usual twenty eight days and the facts had to be binding, there could be no mistakes otherwise the case would not be granted an appeal hearing. Facts, proof, witnesses. Anything to establish that Louise couldn't have killed Alex Turner. New information that would stand the test of cross examination was imperative.

Alan decided to ring George that evening; it had been some time since they spoke and wanted to update him of his new information. He wanted George to know he was working flat out and things were going well.

'Hi George! It's Alan. I've found a few things out you'll be interested in. Are you sitting down?'

'Hi Alan, I am now, fire away.'

'Alex is not the father of Susannah's baby; it's Philip Scott.'

'How on earth did you get that information Alan?' He didn't wait for a reply 'Surely that's a good motive to get Alex out of the way.'

'Yes, it is, but we need more George. The court will say that they could have just divorced. To appeal we need more information. I have to place either Susannah or even Philip at the crime scene.'

'But they could afford to get a hit man to do the job for them.'

'You're right, George, and I have a few friends making inquiries about that. There aren't that many professional killers and most are known in the underworld of crime. We'll just have to wait on that.'

'Oh, there's something else. It seems that William Hopkins is in favour of the couple's new relationship. He's going to set them up in a firm of their own. It makes me wonder how much he knows or maybe even helped with the disposal of Alex Turner. Some of these high flying Lawyers often sail close to the wind. They think they're above the law and know far too

135

many criminals who can be bought, having represented most of them through the years.'

George tried to be helpful by putting his angle on the possibilities. 'From another point of view, Alan; maybe Alex found out about their relationship and confronted them. He may have threatened to publicly disgrace them.' He was eager to nail the pair and free his girl and, in fairness, he had added to the pot; Alan hadn't thought of that.

'Maybe you could visit Louise soon, George, and ask her if Alex ever told her of any suspicions he may have had. But for now we'll think on all that. Have a good night's sleep knowing we are getting somewhere.'

'Thanks Alan.' Both men sat for a while each looking at their telephones, miles apart but both on the same mission.

Chapter 21

Problems at Lockwood Park.

Louise was desperate to see her dad again he had become her only hope of getting out of this place and ending her nightmare. On the wing the problems were escalating between Louis and Tracy. None of which were Louise's fault. It seemed that Tracy would create conflict within her own mind as if there were two people inside her. There would be nasty arguments that would spring from nowhere and often get physical. It was exhausting. At times, Tracy was surreal. She'd change from being her usual arrogant but placid self to a maniac flying at Louise with such contempt and anger it even changed the way she looked. Her face would be contorted and she'd snarl with tight lips and piercing eyes. At times like that Louise was in fear for her own safety.

Louise would mostly leave the cell and take refuge on the landing where she knew Tracy rarely went.

'You need to report her behaviour, Louise; she'll kill you one day.' Jan was fearful for her friend.

'Either the drugs have caused paranoia or she's schizophrenic. Whatever it is she needs help, you can't hide it anymore Louise.'

Jan was, of course, right.

On one occasion Tracy was so angry, again over nothing. She threw Louise against the door and then tried to cut her own body with a plastic comb. Slicing at her wrists until she drew blood. Prison guards restrained her and a doctor was called to tranquilise her. After that episode she had a few days in the hospital wing. Louise prayed she wouldn't come back but she did. For some reason Tracy was much calmer and without outbursts. Louise believed she was medicated although no-one said anything.

Maybe now there would be peace in their cell and Louise wouldn't have to live in fear. Most importantly to Louise, she hadn't reported her. It was strange, but as time went on Louise began to have sympathy for her cellmate. Tracy knew that Louise and her dad were talking again; but she still had no-one.

Visiting day had arrived and Louise decided not to upset her father by telling him about Tracy. Sitting in the visiting hall waiting to see his face at the door was exciting. She couldn't contain her emotions as he walked towards her; she sprung up and ran to his arms.

They held each other for a while and George was aware of his daughter's frame becoming thinner, she seemed so tiny.

'Are you eating sweetheart?'

'I'm fine, Dad, any news?'

They held hands across the table as George related all the details of Alan's investigation.

'You have a private investigator? I can't believe you would do all this for me after the way I've treated you Dad.'

'I hurt you love, but I never stopped loving you.'

There was a few seconds silence as George got his thoughts together.

'Alan wants to know if Alex ever gave you the impression that he suspected Susannah of having an affair with Philip Scott.'

'We never spoke of her, never. Alex worked so hard on the kennels he was building that we only saw each other when I went there under some pretence. I was such a fool dad.' Louise deviated and George held her hand whilst she spoke, understanding her pain and frustration. 'When I look back, the love I believed we had was all in my own imagination. Although he said things that implied I was his true love I can see now that it was all in my head. I just assumed that we'd be together some day. It looks now as if I just filled in some time until Susannah settled in Camberley Edge and they would live the dream together. How could I have been so gullible?'

'Don't think so badly of yourself darling; Alex took advantage of a young and trusting young girl. We'll sort this mess out and you'll soon be home with us.'

Sadly, Louise had no information that could help. George told her to think about everything that was said between them. Maybe something would come back to her, anything at all.

George's heart was breaking as he had to leave his daughter behind in that dreadful prison, but he'd get her out somehow.

The alternative wasn't an option.

Chapter 22

Alan Brings the Case Together.

Alan Preston James, when on such a case, was always at his office before 7am. Today he was waiting for some information from a contact that had promised to ring before 8am. Sitting at his desk waiting for the call, he decided to looks through his notes, rather that waste time. His background in forensic psychology told him to look at the evidence again, and again, then again from other perspectives. Lateral thinking can expose objectives you would otherwise miss.

He was attempting to understand how Susannah's thought process worked and what she was capable of. To do this he needed to ask himself questions. Could she shoot down the man she claimed she loved? Was she callous enough to have taken Philip Scott as her lover when Alex had moved into Jasmine Cottage permanently? Maybe the affair had started earlier. So many maybes.

Alan decided to focus on the facts and what he knew to be true. It seems that she has always used her maiden name for the purpose of work but since the demise of her husband she has reverted to using it at all times. The world believes that her child is the daughter of Alex Turner but Alan now knows differently. He wondered how she could live with herself. If everyone knows that she has moved on and Philip Scott is now a firm part of her life, why doesn't she admit he's the father openly? At the very least to her parents; or maybe they do know and told her to bide her time. These are all very clever people and enjoy getting their own way. Speculation is good and often turns ideas into facts but he had to get some firm facts to work with, and find some new ones. A good appeal case must be solid, you only get one chance.

The telephone rang, breaking the silence in his office.

The information he needed was coming in fast and it was now his job to put the pieces of the jigsaw together. Alan was grateful that his endeavours in fact-finding were progressing as they were. Believing that Susannah was guilty was one thing but getting the facts to support that belief was another. The only way to prepare a case for appeal is to establish major, factual differences to the original trial; and that was not easy.

Susannah was no ordinary criminal. Alan was relying on her confidence to be her downfall. She may have the belief that her expertise in law would equip her to be the perfect criminal but everyone makes mistakes and Alan has to find Susannah's.

Alan believed that, at the time of inquiry, Susannah had the expectation that no-one would analyse her as a potential murderer and calculate her motivation for such an expeditious crime. Her assumption being that the murder of her husband whilst pregnant with his child would be inconceivable. There is also her unblemished character and the prodigious family history and heritage, as yet untarnished.

Susannah also relied on the asinine assumption that she could have committed the murder considering her projection of the fact that she was as much a victim as her dead husband.

All could possibly have made good sense at the time, especially when the prefect suspect was standing by in the form of Louise.

Charging Louise was certainly the more obvious path to take at that time.

With all the new evidence that Alan was uncovering the tables were beginning to turn and Susannah was replacing Louise as the prime suspect.

There was still more work to do to make the case worthy of appeal. Alan had to come up with another angle of attack.

So that's what he worked on for the rest of the day.

Chapter 23

The Hopkins Family Move On.

No-one but Susannah knew how difficult it was for a girl to be raised by William Hopkins. But, in more recent years he had become less stern and supported her well after the loss of Alex. After the tearful funeral of her husband; pregnant Susannah never returned to Camberley Edge but stayed permanently at the London apartment with plans to continue to work at Benjamin, Scott, Walters & Parsons until her maternity leave expires. Susannah had a healthy pregnancy giving birth to her 7lb 9oz baby daughter Eva-Lucy several months later.

Her parents, Isabel and William, tried to get her to rent out the apartment and live in the family home in Kent, with them for support, but she wanted so much to be independent and not go back to square one. However, after a while Susannah conceded realising that she needed her family to help with the child and moved in with them, keeping the apartment free. Philip wasn't happy but if Susannah was to go back to work full time she had no alternative and, as far as he was concerned, that seemed to be the plan. Her maternity leave was running out fast and she had to make a decision about where her future lay, as a full time mother or to go back to work.

When Eva-Lucy was only a few months old Susannah had began to get restless. Motherhood was wonderful but, in her opinion, could be more wonderful if it was part time. She knew she had to make a stand but didn't expect it to be easy.

Dinner was being served at the Hopkins' mansion. William Jnr and Susannah sat with their parents making light conversation when Susannah took the floor.

'Mother!' Susannah got her attention between the main course and pudding.

'I want to go back to work full time and live in my apartment.'

She now had the attention of her father too.

'Susannah, darling! You have a child and all you need with us. Your place is here, now you're a mother. How could you possibly cope in London with a child and working? It's just too ridiculous for words.' Isabel gave an exaggerated sigh and William took over.

'Your mother was home with you and William. And rightly so. You should do the same, young lady.' William always nodded his head to accentuate his point when he spoke and believed he was right. It was an annoying to those who looked on.

Isabel softened as she saw the distress in her daughter face. She recalled herself at that age, also charged with giving up her legal profession to raise her children under the guidance of a dominant husband. She saw the look of despair on her daughter's face and understood exactly how she was feeling. Isabel had done what she was told by William all her life but she could see thc pain in her daughter and had to speak up for her.

'Things have changed since our day, darling.' Isabel said lightly looking at William. Isabel recognised something in her daughter that she never had, determination to succeed. She touched Susannah's hand across the table giving her encouragement to continue.

'I love Eva so much but I love my work too, daddy. Is that so wrong? Is it wrong to want both?' She aimed those questions at her father.

'No, of course not' William conceded hesitantly 'but how can you take Eva to the city with you? Who will care for her when you are at work? A stranger?'
'William,' Isabel, for once in her life spoke firmly to her husband. 'Perhaps Eva could live with us and Susannah could come home as often as work would allow.'

'Is that what you want darling?' William's voice softened when he saw his lovely daughter's tears. Isabel was pleased to see that William was mellowing with age, it suited him.

'Yes dad, I really want to get back to work. Could you help me with Eva?'

'Of course we can. Can't you, Isabel?' They all laughed as pudding was served.

William remained silent, almost pensive, and then suddenly interrupted the others as they enjoyed their fruit salad and ice cream.

'Su, sweetheart. I've been thinking of late.'

'Oh no, not of late!' Isabel ridiculed.

William held up his hand, commanding attention.

'No no, really. I'd like to extend my firm into the city. Of course my name would head the partnership as usual; well, that may sound unnecessary when I say I'm looking at Hopkins & Hopkins as a name. What do you think Susannah?'

'Do you mean it daddy, really? In the city?'

'Yes I do, it's time the family made its mark in the city.'

William smiled, that contented sort of smile when a plan comes together.

A decision was made that Susannah would return to Benjamin, Scott, Walters & Parsons for up to a year or at least until an office in a prime location could be found and all other details put in place.

From that evening onwards, William Hopkins had a purpose. He had work to do.

The business of law was a complicated issue and for a good firm of lawyers it was important to build a worthy reputation. Interviews would have to be planned for various positions. William smiled to himself knowing he always got exactly what he wanted. For the time being he was satisfied that with good lawyers and administrative staff in place, after a while, he could step back and allow Susannah to take the reigns.

Eva-Lucy was growing fast and both William and Isabel enjoyed their time with her, but weekends when Susannah was home was the best; the whole family would be together.

Philip and Susannah had tried to keep their relationship as discreet as possible at first. Many who speculated stood in judgement quietly spreading the gossip until it was all over the legal sector. Now it was second hand news and no-one really cared.

It didn't take long for the couple to take advantage of Susannah's nights in the city and get back to their old routine. Philip and Susannah would spend nights together at her apartment. They even travelled into work together, challenging the gossip and it worked.

Susannah hated letting her parents believe that Eva-Lucy was Alex's child but would have to admit adultery if she confessed and that would change everything. Lately her conscience was getting the better of her.

'I think we should tell my parents and get it over with regardless of the consequences. I can't stand the thought of deceiving them any longer Phil.'

'Don't be hasty, my love. We should take things easy.' Philip was only too aware of what that would really mean and didn't want to take the chance.

'Surely you want to be a real father to Eva-Lucy and see her every day. Popping in and out of her life like an uncle isn't what I want for her.'

'Lets enjoy this evening and we'll talk about it tomorrow. I love you Suzy and don't you forget it.'

He took her in his arms and looked lovingly into her beautiful blue eyes. His obvious manipulation seemed to escape Susannah's notice as she melted against his body. Thinking only of how she loved him and how things would be. Phil was good at getting what he wanted; a tall good-looking guy, intelligent and always saying the right thing both in the court room and the bedroom. He was everything a man needed to be, a catch, and he knew it. Susannah would sometimes be angry at his arrogance and self obsession. Solipsism in the true sense; a man who only recognised himself and his own needs. Mostly she ignored that side of his nature as he was so very good at using the right words which made her feel special and totally loved. Undoubtedly a mistake on her part. Susannah also decided that the paternity of her daughter would never be mentioned again, Eva-Lucy was hers and it didn't really matter who her father was.

Both Philip and Susannah were on call as criminal advocates which meant many cosy evenings would be disrupted by calls from clients who had been arrested at all hours. They had their own clients but shared the new ones and often flipped a coin to see who would turn up for the call.

Phil relented to Susannah's demands and started visiting her parents with her at weekends. When Isabel realised there were midnight manoeuvres from one room to another she broached the subject of room sharing.

'Susannah darling! You really should be honest about these matters. We are all adults; you're not a teenager any more. If you want to share your bedroom that's your business. I suspect that's the situation in the city anyway.'

'What about daddy though?'

'You leave your father to me, sweetheart. I've managed him for many years.'

Philip and Susannah rarely spoke of Alex together, in some ways pretending he never existed. Individually, his memory plagued them both with thoughts of their betrayal of him and ultimately his demise. Philip seemed to shake off the feelings of guilt more easily than Susannah. There was no doubt that Susannah had loved him once, he was so different to every other, so fresh and unspoilt. An eager young man with dreams and plans for a wonderful future for himself and the woman he loved. That in itself was doomed with his choice of wife. Susannah wanted familiarity and a glamorous life in the city but she did try to please him. The answer for them both was finding love in the arms of another; not only making everything ten times worse but fatal.

Philip was more Susannah's type, what she had been brought up to expect from a man; a man just like daddy. He fitted into the life she knew and he began to spend more and more time with the Hopkins' at their home, getting on with one and all.

It was getting more emotionally difficult for Susannah to leave Eva-Lucy after spending the weekend with her. She was as beautiful as her mother with her big blue eyes and white blonde hair. Susannah never gave a second thought about Alex's parents but they constantly thought about the child they believed to be their granddaughter. Losing Alex broke their heart but not seeing Eva-Lucy was unbearable. Isabel realised that may be the case and wanted to help, she hadn't spoken to Shan since Alex's funeral but had written and sent photos when the little girl was born. Susannah never mentioned them so Isabel was discrete, she didn't want to upset her daughter.

As a grandmother she felt it was time to reach out to Shan and Bryn so she invited them to come and see Eva-Lucy and stay over night.

The letter pleased Shan but she had reservations as to how she would cope with the emotions.

'I don't know if I can do it, Bryn, just see this precious little girl now and again. It will break my heart to leave her. When I hold her in my arms I will only think of Alex and what he's missing.'

'We must go, love, for Alex's sake, if nothing else. I need to go, Shan.' His eyes were pleading and Shan new he was right so they acknowledged the letter and made preparations for the journey including a boot full of cloths and toys for their little grandchild.

Isabel chose a weeknight for the visit but knew she had to tell Susannah.

'I can't believe you'd go behind my back and invite them, I can't believe it.' Susannah was more upset than Isabel had thought she'd be. 'I allowed them to take Alex's ashes home to Wales; what more do they want?'

'It's their right as grandparents to see her, Su, you can't be that cruel.'

'I want to be here, then.'

It wasn't exactly how Isabel had planned it but there was nothing she could do.'

They arrived around 3pm and Isabel had prepared a snack with plans for a late dinner. She had told Susannah they were expected before dinner so that she wouldn't rush home from work and the Turners would have time alone with Eva-Lucy.

As usual, Isabel was the perfect host. Shan tried to smile and hold back her emotions but the second she held Eva in her arms the tears flowed. Within seconds all four grandparents were as one with love for the precious little girl they all held so dear.

Alex was mentioned but only in regard to things that Shan believed she saw in Eva. Both sets of parents were uncomfortable with the misgivings of their children but showed no contempt for each other; in fact, they behaved as friends.

Just before dinner Susannah walked in. Isabel saw a look in her eye that told her that she had been thinking of this meeting all day. There were few words between Susannah and her in-laws but that was expected. What no one expected was the outburst from Susannah after a few glasses of wine at dinner.

'What do you want from me?' It started and Isabel knew she was powerless to stop her daughters rage. 'Your son ruined my life with his adultery and you expect to see my child?'

'Please, Susannah,' Shan tried to explain, 'please don't hate us. We didn't even know about it. We welcomed you into our family and I loved you because it was clear my son did. I don't know what happened to change things but we love Eva-Lucy and we need to see her from time to time. She needs to know us too.'

'You know nothing.' Susannah was screaming and her cheeks were flushed. 'You know nothing.'

William intervened. 'Well I know something Susannah; your behaviour is unreasonable and disgraceful. We don't need to know about the goings-on between you and Alex but he didn't deserve to die and his parents do not deserve to be spoken to like that. Not in my house.'

Susannah left the room in tears and Bryn made the decision that they would not stay the night.

'But you can't drive all that way at this time of night.' Isabel pleaded.

Bryn continued. 'It was hard for us to come because we knew what our boy did, and it was wrong but he's paid with his life. We'll never understand his actions but there's a child that we all love and we can't ignore her. We'll give Susannah time, all she needs, but eventually we will see Eva; it's our right. Please try to speak with her when she's calm and maybe she'll see sense. If not we'll do what we have to. I don't want to hurt you both but surely you understand?'

'We'll talk to her.' William agreed. 'We'll sort things out and let you know, Bryn.'

The Turners repacked their bags and left for the long journey home.

When Susannah realised they had gone she came back down stairs, still seething.

Isabel was tearful as she spoke. 'My God! Susannah! How could you be so cruel to them? It's not their fault that Alex betrayed you. Perhaps you should take a good look at your behaviour at the time, young lady.'

'How dare you speak to me like that?' Susannah spat the words at her mother.

William took control once more. 'No, Susannah. How dare you? Never speak like that! Your mother is innocent in knowledge of your lifestyle. I dare to speak to you like this because I know a little more about you than you realise, so don't continue this pretence with me. Perhaps Alex found out about you and Philip. Maybe your antics pushed him into the arms of another.'

He looked at his wife; her face said it all. The moment he said the words, he knew there was no going back and he had regrets.

Isabel was clearly annoyed. 'Some things are better left unsaid, William, and you of all people should know that.'

Susannah was leaving the room as her mother spoke and didn't seem to register the implications of what had been said.

Too much was said and yet much was left unsaid. The way of the Hopkins family is to paper over the cracks and carry on with life. A dangerous process. The one thing that was unanimously felt was the care and protection of their precious Eva-Lucy. Her happiness had to be paramount to all else. So life went on, just the same.

William rarely spoke out against his children; to do so would incur the wrath of Isabel who was the glue that held the family together. His way of apologising to them was to offer Philip a partnership in the city practice and adding his name to the firm. William recognised that Susannah and Philip were an item and, despite everything, he liked him. Philip reminded William of himself as a young man. Phil was eager to get on and wasn't afraid to put the hours in; again reminding William of himself in years past. He wanted the decision to be a secret so that he could tell Philip himself.

After dinner one evening when they were all at the house William decided to hold audience and make an occasion of his surprise for Philip. Standing with his back to the fireplace, facing his audience with a brandy in one hand and a large cigar in the other he started.

'Philip, my boy, I've been thinking of your relationship with Susannah.'

Phil got a little nervous, thinking the old boy was about to tell him to move on.

'You are a good man and that's what my daughter needs in her life. A man who has the same ambitions and knows their path in life.'

Phil relaxed a little.

'You've served your firm of solicitors well and work to a high standard whereby you are recognised by many in the city. It is because of Susannah and your exceedingly good work ethics that I would like to offer you a partnership in the city firm.' He took a long breath and continued.

'Well, what are you waiting for boy? Shake my hand and say "thank you".' William smiled and reached out his hand.

Phil stood up instantly and took William's hand.

'Thank you! Thank you so much, sir. I am truly grateful and will work hard to uphold the firm's name and good reputation.' Philip knew immediately what this meant. A firm with the name Hopkins would be regarded as prestigious. Business would come in from the highest levels and the firm would be recognised amongst the very best in the legal profession. His dream had come true.

'Good lad. I have decided that my name will not be above the door as we had planned and I will begin to prioritise my life quite differently. Perhaps this will come as a bit of a shock to my lovely wife but I want to spend my days enjoying life with her before she loses her loveliness.' He laughed, and Isabel smiled sweetly remembering why she had fallen in love with this man and persevered for many years with a sometimes irritating character such as he.

'So the name will now be Hopkins & Scott with Susannah being the managing and senior partner. I'm sure you will accept that for the time being. Maybe one day it will change to Scott & Scott but that is none of my business is it Isabel.' He looked sheepishly at his wife.

Before the champagne was opened to seal the deal in the usual Hopkins manner William had one more thing to announce.

'William, I have something for you too, son.'

William Jnr. looked surprised, this seemed serious.

'I am handing over my local office to you and removing my name from that also.' There was silence.

'But dad you love doing a few days a week; you say it keeps your mind busy.'

'I will be busy son; I'll be enjoying my granddaughter, maybe taking her on holidays. A caravan would be nice; you always loved it as children.'

'I think this is where I step in darling.' Isabel smiled.

'A caravan, at my age, maybe not. But I am delighted that, for once in your life, you are taking some time for us.'

A magnum of Crystal was enjoyed by all and, it seemed, life was good.

William spoke with Mr Benjamin from Philip's firm and Philip could be released to start work with Susannah when the organisation of the new practice was complete. William Hopkins had known Stephen Benjamin for many years and understood that he was coming to the end of his working career; a generous cheque passing from one friend to another softened the blow of losing Phil and ensured a good transition with no hard feelings. Stephen even told William that he would transfer Phil's work to the new firm as a gesture of good will. That would stand them in good stead for the coming year and repeat business there after.

Philip knew he was at the start of something big; a turning point in his life. He would have liked to be an equal partner but he could work on that. Sometimes, his determination to achieve at everything was a little overpowering but it was the only way he knew. Knowing what he wanted and determination in getting it, made him a formidable opponent; but Philip Scott was never satisfied. He always wanted more.

Chapter 24

Susannah Builds the Team.

Whilst Louise languishes in prison, Susannah enjoys her new life.

The excitement of building a new team of solicitors from scratch was a challenge. Susannah was ready for the next phase in her life.

She knew it wouldn't be easy finding a full team of legal staff of the high standard that the reputation of the Hopkins name demands. There couldn't be newly trained lawyers on the team it would be time wasting to nurture kids straight out of university who would inevitably make mistakes and risk the reputation of the firm. They all had to be specialists in their field to match the opposition that was prevalent in the London legal sector. It was common that advocates slid from one firm to another when there were unlimited financial rewards for doing so but it would still be difficult to find a good working team. The only problem Susannah had was that her father insisted on being on the interview team and he was a formidable character. He always got his way. Those were the conditions and she had no choice but to comply.

So the interviews were planned. Word was put out that a new firm was about to be launched under the name of Hopkins & Scott and applications flooded in. Susannah thought hard about the profile that would suit her plans and had come up with quite a simple idea. It would give the law firm a unique modus operandi. No-one over forty years of age; of course, that couldn't be advertised but there are always ways around it. William wasn't happy about it but was willing to see what was on offer within that age bracket. In his mind it was obvious that experience is always a good thing for a lawyer to have and that comes only with time. However, he could also see that in Susannah and Philip, both young, there was energy, enthusiasm and hunger which had motivated them both to become the best in their field. He also recognised that they were both quite unique and decided to go along with their idea for the moment. Ageism, sexism and many more isms are illegal so the over forties that would qualify would have to receive a brief interview for the sake of appearance. They would receive a 'so sorry but on this occasion you were unsuccessful' letter and their CVs would be binned thereafter. Of that Susannah was firm; she was certainly her father's daughter.

Susannah, as senior partner would also be group manager. In theory, she would manage the practise but, in reality the mundane side of her role could be allocated to a good administrator. Most firms would recruit a practice manager but Susannah needed to feel she had control at least until the practice was on its feet and working well.

Legal aid was mandatory for a city firm and all aspects of law were soon covered by under forty year olds. Susannah and Philip were experts in criminal law and would be able to cover both youth work and adult. Philip had been the criminal law expert when Susannah had joined the firm of Benjamin,Scott,Walters & Parson. She soon became his protégée, learning everything from Philip but in most ways surpassing his expertise. This supported her belief in her inherently successful nature.

The team was ready to be put to work exactly as Susannah had envisaged, they were all under forty years of age. William was surprised but pleased that all applicants seemed right for their positions and, although a little reluctant, he stepped back and let the new team get on with the hard work.

Legal secretaries and general clerical staff were needed too but easier to find. An agency was always the best place to start and positions were filled quickly.

A good receptionist would be the next important member of staff. It's the first person a client would meet when they come into the office so she would have to be smart and articulate. Susannah was clear on what she wanted.

Philip trusted Susannah's judgement and was content to let her make the decisions. She interviewed a few potential receptionists from the agency but none were what she was looking for. An advertisement was placed in newspapers and CVs were coming in fast. Susannah rejected most of them. Only a couple were worth interviewing so a date was set when Susannah could interview the potential applicants.

One in particular had an exceptionally good reference and soon became the only realistic option. Susannah interviewed them and made her decision over- night that it was to be the young lady who had stood out from the beginning.

Deborah Collings was appointed. She was able to start the following Monday and, on the condition that her references were what she had claimed, she would then receive a full contract after three months. Both parties were pleased.

Deborah was 5 foot 6 inches with a deliciously curvaceous body, as Phil had already noted on her first day at the office. Her long black hair had an Asian appearance, black, and straight and with a lovely shine. But more than that she was well spoken, albeit with a slight accent which was difficult to place. Deborah had no fear of showing the couple that she needed and wanted the job promising them her full commitment.

Deborah was desperate to get the job and would prove her worth. Not many girls of her young age had such a confident manner and, above all, she turned out to be a quick learner who was prepared to work longer days when needed. In a short period of time Deborah became an asset to the firm. Her work ethic turned out to be exactly what she had promised in interview and her references supported everything she had said. She soon became a respected part of the team.

The conveyance solicitor, Simon Dent, came with good credentials and reminded Susannah a little of Alex. He was eager to please which meant that he could be moulded to suit the culture of the firm; Susannah wanted the firm to have a reputation for conscientiousness and reliability, a must in the eye of a Hopkins.

It wasn't long before the full team of lawyers were working flat out. Their energetic youth and determination shone through and Susannah was proud of her choices. New business was coming in fast and there weren't many days when there was time to spare. Susannah worked well with Deborah and slowly began to rely on her to manage the clerical staff and their work. The typists and legal secretaries were good at their job, especially in the support they gave to the legal team. It was always Susannah's intension to maintain a business relationship with her staff, something her father had taught her. There was never individual favouritism shown and professionalism at all times. Susannah always discussed staff salary privately with each but their previous experience, qualities and dedication to the firm equated to top salaries for all.

Susannah always felt a little disappointed when Philip flouted these standards and seemed to want to make friends with the staff. It was unethical and so annoying to her when he chatted to one more than another and clearly had his favourites amongst the females. Often there would be arguments between the couple regarding his over enthusiasm with the female staff in the workplace. He never understood why Susannah had such silly rules and mostly ignored them.

'I don't understand why you have such intense conversations with the staff about things that shouldn't concern them, Phil.'

'I'm just sociable, Su. You should try it sometime.' His response was even more annoying.

'You have to see it from my point of view though.' Susannah tried to ignore his ridicule. 'It's not good that they see a weakness and I'm concerned that your behaviour could be construed as flirting. I know our relationship is strong but these young girls may be flattered by your attention.'

'You do your thing and I'll do mine, Miss Perfect.' Sometimes his words hurt Susannah but her anger with him never lasted long.

Criminal law was always the most demanding on a solicitors' time, mostly because of the out of hours work involved. Susannah went to her parent's home some week nights, so Philip accepted the majority of the evening calls, for which Susannah was grateful and tried to show appreciation to him as best she could. When they were at the London apartment together things were good between them. Sometimes they would go out for dinner. Their mobile phones always accompanied them just in case one or the other were needed to attend a police station to represent a client but it never stopped them enjoying the London night life.

Philip never mentioned Alex or his demise, in the belief that it may cause Susannah to relive the sadness of the past. It had been a difficult time in their lives when the details of his murder were being investigated. The police seemed to think that the whole incident was cut and dried. All the evidence pointed to Louise. No one else was even considered. There was so much the police didn't know and even more that they didn't consider as relevant. Some would say a shambles but for Susannah it turned out well. Her parents were devastated at the loss of their son-in-law and the heartbreak of his affair. They were there for Susannah in her hour of need and supported her in every way they could. For Susannah, she was simply relieved and extremely pleased that the whole episode was over and she could live her life again without the fear of what might have been.

Alex's parents were grateful to Susannah for letting them have his ashes to take him home to Wales. They struggled on with their lives but their hearts were broken. Not only with the loss of their son but the possibility of never knowing their granddaughter. Susannah seemed unfairly resentful of them. Bryn and Shan were as disgusted by their son's adultery with that young girl as Susannah was. They spent many an evening in front of the fire in their farm house in Landrindod Wells in silence but both with the same thoughts. How could their son have done such a thing? Where had they gone wrong as parents? There were no answers. Not, at least, for the time being anyway.

Even after their rejection by Susannah and her outburst when they visited to see Eva-Lucy the Turners continued to maintain contact with Isabel Hopkins. Isabel was a kind person and had sympathy for their situation. Her daughter was behaving in an exceptionally bad way and Isabel went behind Susannah's back to try and make amends. She took pictures of everything the little girl did and sent copies to her Welsh grandparents. Shan was so grateful to receive those photos. Her Welsh dresser in the kitchen, a family heirloom, was covered in framed photos of the child that was so precious to them. The only thing left of their son and his short life.

Chapter 25

Louise Begins to Struggle.

The excitement of seeing her father again, after such a long time had kept her spirits up. Louise knew that he would do everything he could to free her from her torment of incarceration. Sometimes, bad thoughts would crowd her mind and she was helpless to escape them. It was difficult to pray to a God that seemed to have deserted her. The times between visits left her feeling isolated; George realised this. She would be so happy when she saw him walk into the visiting hall, but every visit, as they hugged; George noticed that she became thinner and frailer.

The inmates would only leave their wing for recreation and chapel. The security was tight for the secure, long term offenders so they didn't meet with other prisoners. Their confinement was sometimes total isolation if they were considered dangerous or vulnerable. Louise was beginning to understand prison life. The monotony of the every day rituals would take the women's will and alter their minds.

Louise had grown to hate the early mornings when the lights would come on suddenly; they were bright and relentless. After a night of dark thoughts and bad dreams it seemed cruel to be forced from your bed when you'd just fallen asleep.

It is clear that the percentage of inmates with mental disorders is exceedingly high sometimes due to reaction to drug taking or the need for it; both cases are prevalent in prison situations.

The guards may appear passive but are trained to deal with any arguments quickly and confine the trouble makers to their cells for a period of time, sometimes losing their privileges which are of major importance to these women who have little or nothing. Louise is more comfortable with the peaceful times when the days drift from one to another without conflict.

When a new woman arrives there's always excitement. If the offence is high profile she's even more popular. If there are any prisoners with sole occupancy of a double cell things get difficult. No one wants to share with a 'newbie' especially if it's her first time inside; they always cry a lot. Louise was just like that, she recalled. There were terrible arguments between her and Tracy because of her sobbing at night. Eventually, Louise's nocturnal tears subsided but she never stops thinking of getting out of the place and still has hope of freedom, especially now her dad is on the scene and most importantly he believes she's innocent. Even though she feels the whole world is against her.

Proving her innocence will be hard. Louise spends every waking moment going over things that had happened before Alex's death and mostly coming up with nothing. There must be something she's overlooking and she tries to recall her intimate times with Alex. Dredging every word he had said from the depths of her memories. They rarely spoke of Susannah and she kept a low profile in the village, speaking only to one or two neighbours when confronted by them in the streets.

On a few occasions Susannah had actually rung Alex's mobile phone when Louise had been with him. He always indicated for her to be quiet and she mostly crept into another room but couldn't help but listen to their conversation. It always seemed that they were happy by the things they said and when the conversation between them came to an end he always whispered 'I love you' and made silly little kissing noises down the phone. It broke Louise's heart.

Louise felt sure, at that time, that Susannah had no idea about the relationship she was having with her husband. Now she felt differently and was beginning to believe that woman was capable of keeping the knowledge to herself until the right moment. When her dad told her that Philip Scott was the baby's father Louise was even more convinced that Susannah wanted a way out of her marriage and Louise was exactly what she needed, a scapegoat. All Louise knew for a fact was that she hadn't killed Alex; she mistakenly believed they even had a future together and Alex was just biding his time.

It had to be Susannah, of that Louise was certain, who else could it be? Who else had the tenacity to formulate such a plan as to kill her own husband and frame someone else? It was probable that Susannah had somehow discovered her husband's betrayal, his infidelity. It was also possible that Philip was a part of it all. Louise's mind was working overtime. She tried hard to remain focussed; it was no good speculating, that wouldn't get her any where.

Would Philip have wanted a paternity test to prove his fatherhood? The fact that Alex thought the baby was his, indicated a normal sex life between him and Susannah. Did she tell Philip this was not the case? It must be concluded that Susannah was promiscuous if she had gone from her marital bed into the arms of her lover. So what more is she capable of?

So much was going on in Louise's desperate thoughts but there must have been things done or said that would help her dad prove her innocence. If only she knew what.

It was unusual, but for once Louise was alone in her cell. She lay on her bunk grateful for the clean, smoke free air and freedom from the anxiety that being with Tracy gave her. It was strangely quiet and she wondered how Tracy was, in the hospital wing. During the night Louise had been awoken by gasping sounds coming from Tracy's bed. She suddenly realised Tracy was having an asthma attack and called for a guard. Louise had never seen such a thing before but knew Tracy was asthmatic as she used a pump often and was even allowed to keep it with her, just in case. Tracy was almost blue from lack of oxygen as she tried to gasp in some air and Louise was visibly distressed as she watched Tracy being taken out of the cell and down to the hospital wing. When they had settled Tracy, a guard Louise knew as Jo came back to let her know that Tracy was fine and recovering in the hospital wing. Of course, Louise was pleased to hear the good news but that didn't stop her enjoying her time alone.

In the silence Louise drifted off to sleep; her dreams were always about Alex and the happy times they shared; walking the dogs behind his house and evenings of love when his wife stayed in the city. She woke with tears and heartache. That happened a lot but it was better than not remembering him at all.

It must have been only minutes later when Louise woke again with all sorts of rubbish rolling around her mind. She decided to get up and went over to the basin and threw some cold water over her face; she was mentally exhausted.

There was little sleep that night for Louise and, as usual, just as she dropped off the lights came on. The bell rang and the doors unlocked. Sleepily she got up and brushed her teeth and dressed. Leaving her cell she walked with the others to collect her breakfast. There was some morning chatter but Louise remained silent with her thoughts making a mental note to ask her father on visiting day to pop into the house to see if there was mail. It had just dawned on her that there would be bills to pay and most importantly the mortgage. It was probably so much in arrears that the cottage may even have been repossessed. Better still she would telephone him during 'association' that night. Prisoners were entitled to have a PIN in order to make outside telephone calls to numbers registered to their prison number. The costs were high, about 30 pence per minute but she had some money on her account.

Later that day, after supper, she stood in line for the telephone. There were six women in the queue but thankfully they didn't have a lot of credit on their cards so her turn came around quickly.

'Hi dad. How are you?' It felt good that she had someone to ring.

'Hi darling. This is a surprise.'

'I hope a good surprise.'

'Of course! I love to hear from you. Is there something wrong sweetheart?'

'No, not really, just something I need you to do for me. Can you go to Madge's on Saturday on your way to see me? I know it's out of your way but it's important. She has a house key and I need you to see if there's mail regarding the mortgage repayments. They must be so overdue.'

'Of course I will love; I must admit I hadn't given that any thought.'

'Dad, I have to go. This call is costing me a fortune. Oh! One more thing, as you are going into the house, can you bring me some jeans and sweaters. I can have up to ten items but you'll have to make a request to bring them in. I've been wearing other prisoners cast-offs because I had no one on the outside.'

'I'll do that, sweetheart. Take care of yourself darling. I love you.'

'I love you too, dad.'

The phone went silent. Louise held it in her hand for a few seconds more. It was hard to say good-bye. A thud in her back from the next girl in line brought her back to reality.

Rather than just turn up on Madge's doorstep George decided to ring her first.

'Hello Madge! It's George Anderson.'

'Hello, George! What can I do for you?' The response was definitely not warm.

'I've just had a call from Louise.' George kept to the point.

'I didn't know prisoners could phone people on the outside.'

'Well, it's a complicated process. You have to give your consent as a recipient and it's extremely costly but Louise was concerned that there may be mail at the house and she's asked me to collect it before I visit her on Saturday. She said you have a key, Madge.'

'Yes I do have a key but I must admit I haven't been able to go into the house myself since I found Daphne; it was such a shock. I'm sure it needs cleaning George.'

'Don't worry about that. I can understand that it must have been a dreadful for you, finding Daphne as you did. I'll try to be there by 11am which will give me plenty of time to have lunch and get to Louise by 2 pm'

'Okay, George. I'll see you outside the house at 11am on Saturday then.'

'Thank you Madge.'

George felt a little sad that Madge didn't seem to trust him to collect the key and go to the house himself. He understood but it still hurt his pride. After all, he had known Madge for many years.

Abigail and George set off early that Saturday morning, a bit apprehensive about the meeting with Madge and how it would go. The telephone conversation between them had been short but polite so maybe their meeting would be the same.

At the house they saw Madge waiting and Abigail decided to stay in the car, she didn't want a confrontation. It was exactly 11.00 am George got out of the car and walked up the path towards Madge.

'Good morning, George! It's good to see you,' the reception from Madge was warmer than George had expected considering the telephone conversation.

'Hello Madge, you look well. Thanks for helping me sort out things for Louise. I'm very grateful for your help. I have to accept the way you feel about me, I know I've been a disappointment to all my old friends but you've been a good friend to Daphne and for that I can't thank you enough.'

'She took your leaving badly George, especially your relationship with Abigail Flint. You gave up everything for that girl, George. Was it all worth it?'

Madge looked at the car where Abigail waited, but returned her gaze to George's face quickly when she saw Abigail looking at her through the car window.

'I didn't want things to happen the way they did and I take full responsibility. I accept that it's all my fault. Abigail is not the person people think she is, but no-one seemed to want to get to know that side of her.'

Madge's response was curt and to the point. 'Well, that's your business now, George, and you have to live the rest of your life knowing the damage you've done, but at least you're stepping up to the mark with Louise. What she's done is unforgivable but at least she has you back in her life. The sad thing about all this mess concerning Alex Turner is that it probably wouldn't have happened if you had been there. Perhaps things wouldn't have gone so far if there had been some fatherly care and advice from you regarding that man and his high and mighty wife. Or should I say widow?' They stood in silence for a few seconds.

'We never see her in Camberley Edge now and that suits everyone. Anyway, George, you're her to collect the mail so let's go in.'

George couldn't help being hurt by Madge's harsh words but there seemed no point in arguing. Instead George touched Madge's arm gently.

'She didn't kill him, Madge.'

Madge turned around to face George; he stood his ground and looked straight into her eyes and waited, he wanted to see her reaction, to understand her thoughts.

'She was found guilty in a court of law so stop trying to get my sympathy George. She did it and that's that. Then to make things ten times worse, Daphne took her own life because of it.'

George ignored the easy way Madge was so convinced of Louise's guilt.'

'They were wrong and I have to prove her innocence Madge. I've retained the services of a private investigator who actually believes that Susannah killed Alex.'

George waited for Madge's reaction. It was shock; amazement.

'Really? You believe that Louise was framed or something?' It was all a bit Agatha Christie but Madge began to wonder if he could be right. George was a clever man and he seemed convinced. An act of fatherly love perhaps, or even guilt over what he had done. Madge had known George for years, since childhood, and if he believed Louise was innocent then maybe there was a slim chance that she had been mis-judged. It happens; you hear about it on the news all the time. Madge was not totally convinced but George was, and he was no push-over, an educated man with a good understanding of human nature.

165

'I really do believe that Louise was framed, Madge, and I think I may be able to prove it with the help of this private investigator. Please, Madge, will you help me?'

Madge was slow to respond but George could see she was considering what he had said.

'If you really and truly believe she's innocent, George, then yes I will help you. No one really liked Susannah but when we all heard that Louise had been convicted we didn't give it any more thought. It all seemed to fall into place.' There was so much more to be said, but it would keep for another time. 'Now what mail are you looking for, George?'

George and Madge walked into the house together and gathered up the pile of mail behind the door.

'An arrears letter from the mortgage company, Louise said.'

Madge stopped in her tracks.

'There's no mortgage on the house George. Doesn't Louise know that?'

'What do you mean no mortgage? There must be.' George reacted.

'Well I can assure you there's isn't. Daphne was selling her orchids all over the world as well as the U.K. and made herself quite a lot of money. You look surprised, George.'

'She must have made a lot of money to pay off the mortgage though.' George was indeed surprised.

'Oh yes, she did, and a tidy sum in the bank too. You're ex-wife really came into her own when she recovered from the shock you gave her. Okay, I'm sorry George I shouldn't go on to you like this but that is the truth. Daphne had no mortgage and was very well off besides. I'm surprised that Louise didn't know though; there again she was always too busy with the love rat to listen to anything that Daphne had to say. In fact Daphne had started to look for a bigger property in the village with more ground so that she could extend her business further. She was a very successful woman, George. I wish you could have seen that side of her.'

'She was an amazing woman.' George smiled as Madge continued.

'She certainly was, George. Although I did find it very strange when a letter came to me by post from Daphne. It had all the names and addresses of her customers listed in alphabetical order with telephone numbers next to each one. She wanted me to tell them that she wouldn't be selling any more orchids and to thank them for their business. She explained in the letter that they had been valued customers and deserved to be told rather than written to. Daphne had thought of everything before she took her life George, even down to her customers. I realised I hadn't seen her in a few days, so I ran around to the house immediately and that's when I found her. The door was unlocked; something Daphne never did was to leave her front door open. It was the worst moment of my life. I had never seen a dead person, least of all my best friend. I would never have imagined she was capable of taking her own life like that; not in a million years. Of course she was ill. We all knew that. Her medication made her a little strange, too. There were so many drugs to help her through the day she couldn't even go to court for Louise's trial. She always kept saying that I should tell them to lock her up instead of Louise because she was the guilty one and it was all her fault. She would have blamed anyone but her precious daughter. When I walked into the house that day I called out her name but no-one replied. I went into the lounge and found her sitting in the chair so peacefully. I truly thought she was sleeping until I saw the empty bottle.'

'Was there a letter for Louise?' George interrupted.

'No George, only the one I received by post and that was just to tell her customers she was not supplying them any more.'

They stood together in the kitchen and George looked out into the garden.

'Those are her greenhouses then?'

Yes, Daphne's pride and joy.

'The windows are so dirty. The plants must all be dead now.'

'Dead and gone, just like Daphne.' Madge became tearful and George felt her pain.

'Thank you Madge I must go. I don't want to be late for Louise.'

'George, take this. I think you should have it now.'

Madge handed George the key to the house, he gave her a peck on the cheek and walked to the car. Madge waited until they drove off, before walking to the gate; she didn't want to catch Abigail Flint's eye, not yet. It was too soon.

Chapter 26

George Gives Louise Good News.

George and Abigail continued their journey to the prison mostly in silence. George was pensive but felt a little easier knowing that he seemed to be building bridges with Madge and possibly getting her help with his fight to get his precious daughter out of jail. If anyone was respected for their hard work and honesty in Camberley Edge it was Bob and Madge. George hoped that they could help to convince everyone that Louise hadn't killed Alex and support George's cause.

The relief in knowing that Louise had no money worries gave him a boost and he was looking forward to telling her the good news. No mortgage and a little cash in the bank, George was pleased to be bringing Louise some good news to cheer her up.

Abigail had a good heart and was happy to know that there was hope. She had become his rock. Now that Madge was prepared to help, George was even more hopeful. He decided to ring her on the Sunday and ask her if she could ask around the village if anyone had seen or heard anything. If they could see Madge was changing her mind about Louise's guilt then maybe they would do the same. Someone, somewhere will have that small piece of information, perhaps evidence, to put Susannah firmly in the frame and Louise would then be free.

The journey to HMP Lockwood Park was a long one and their old car was not the best. It was a very old Ford Fiesta that had known better days. Abigail had chosen it as a surprise for George not long after they had to sell his Lexus; how he loved his Lexus. The Fiesta would do for now but the noise of the engine was not good and George prayed that it would just hold on for a few months more.

It had started to rain heavily and the windscreen wipers were struggling. The rhythm was annoying because there was a bump every time it hit the side panel of the windscreen. The rhythmic noise was difficult to ignore and there was no radio to listen to and take their mind off the cars problems.

After a short silence, Abigail broke the monotony by asking. 'Did Madge mention me or dad?'

'No, love. We were so busy talking about Louise and her financial situation.' George wanted to protect Abi's feelings but he knew that Madge had seen Abi in the car. The two women had exchanged glances, but Madge offered no more. Even before Madge and Bob found out about his affair with Abigail they disliked her because of her reputation of being a seductress. Of course, she wasn't, but their post office was a hub for gossip and both Bob and Madge were taken in by the tales they had heard.

George also had concerns himself about running into Edward Flint. The last time he saw Edward he'd thrown him over the bonnet of a car. If it hadn't been for Bob goodness knows what would have happened. George was not a fighting man and had no idea how to protect himself. These were all sad memories that maybe in time could be erased, but for now, he had to be concerned with Louise.

It took more than two hours to get to the prison, with only twenty minutes to go before visiting time. George was grateful that Abigail had decided to keep him company for the journey and thought to make a few sandwiches. They pulled into the car park and enjoyed their lunch together. The ham and tomato sandwiches went down well with the flask of hot tea Abigail had brought too. George had to have at least ten cups of tea every day. Abigail teased him that it was a throwback to the time when he had to sit with his parishioners drinking it all day.

The visiting order was only for George so Abi stayed in the car watching as George walked over to the entrance. She had prepared for a long wait by bringing a few magazines.

George hated the procedure that he had to go through to get to his daughter. It was degrading and embarrassing but he also appreciated that it was essential; he found that out today. After showing his pass he was led, with the other visitors, through the security system of rooms. It seemed to George a little like airport control with a surly officer guiding a wand over his body to detect things that shouldn't be there. Personal items had to be put into a locker and collected on the way out, but visitors often tried to smuggle things in.

George was told, never asked, to remove his trouser belt and shoes which were examined carefully and returned to him. He often wondered if he would have been treated any differently had he turned up in his dog collar; he had a few left from his days as the vicar of Camberley Edge.

He hated the chair most of all. Not sitting on it. That was easy. It was the thought of how any one would or even could carry things into the prison within their body. It was made of perforated steel and for some unknown reason was strangely painted a yellow colour. Some kind of detector was underneath the seat and would buzz loudly if it sensed something.

Then there was the Labrador dog who would sit quietly; seemingly oblivious to his role in all this. Most of the time he looked as if he was about to fall asleep, but not today. Something had happened, he became focused and alert. Suddenly, he was working and knew exactly what to do. His handler watched him carefully, saying nothing. The man in front of George was well dressed with a smart hair cut; in fact he looked quite respectable, not your usual prison visitor type. It was his turn to stand still as the dog did his job, and he did. He continually circled the man becoming more and more agitated. Suddenly he sat right in front of the man staring at his face. The dog handler, realising the dog had smelled something, distracted the dog by throwing a tennis ball away from the man towards a wall at the far end of the room. The dog ran after his ball with his tail wagging in excitement, totally forgetting all about the man. His whole attention was now on his yellow tennis ball. The distraction method of standing the dog down was the only way of getting him away from his target and clearing the way for officers to take over. If the dog was lucky he may even get a doggy chew for his work.

The man was taken into a room with officers holding each arm. His face was flushed and it can only be assumed that he was carrying drugs in for someone. A frightening and unreal experience for George but the remaining officers continued with the inspection and directed him on and into the visitor's hall.

Standing at the entrance, he looked around for Louise; she was sitting at a table watching the door for her father. George thought she looked pale and seemed to have lost even more weight. Her small face lit up when she saw him and she stood in readiness of his warm embrace.

'Oh dad! It's so good to see you.' She began to cry as he held her to him.

'How are you darling? Are you eating?' He could feel her bones that seemed to have no flesh on them. Her face was drawn and pale; her eyes wide and tired. He could have cried.

'Yes dad, I'm fine.' Louise dismissed his concern.

'I have some really good news Lou, The house is paid for and there's money in the bank for you.'

'What? How can that be?'

'It seems your mum's business of orchid-growing and selling was more lucrative than you thought. She was quite the business woman Lou.'

'So there's no mortgage to worry about?' George could see the relief on her face.

'Yep and money in the bank love. Oh! and by the way Madge has given me the door key. What do you want me to do with it?'

'Move in.' Louise beamed. 'I think it's only right that you and Abigail should live in the house after all you are doing for me. What d'you think dad?' Louise had the biggest smile on her face. 'You're paying rent in Birmingham and travelling all this way to see me. It makes sense doesn't it?

'It certainly does make sense love; I'll speak to Abigail. We have jobs in Birmingham.'

'Is there something I could sign to give you access to mum's money?'

'Power of Attorney you mean?'

'Yes that sounds right. Can you find out what I need to do?'

'I'll find out by my next visit. Now about getting you out; it won't happen quickly, darling. In fact the whole thing will take some time but things are moving in the right direction and I don't want you to worry. In the meantime you must look after yourself and eat more. D'you promise me?'

'Yes, dad. I promise and I love you.'

'I love you too, baby.'

They chatted for the rest of the time, enjoying each others company, even laughing together. George told her about what had happened to the man at security.

'That happens all the time, dad. But the worst one I've heard of was when a woman who had a baby on the mother-and-baby wing let the baby's dad have time with his little boy on the outside.'

'Does that really happen?' George interrupted.

'Oh yes. They share their time with the baby, inside the prison and on the outside. The day he brought the baby back a female security guard took the baby's nappy off and found a plastic bag with drugs in it. If the bag had burst the baby could have ingested the drugs and died.'

George was stunned but before he could say anything the sound of that dreadful bell filled the room telling the visitors it was time to leave.

They hugged once more before George turned and left. Louise struggled to hold back the tears until her dad was out of sight and sound. Then she gave vent to the emotions no-one could ever understand unless they had walked in her shoes. She was coming to the end of her tether and she could feel her strength leaving her. How could she go on?

George couldn't get the face of his beloved Louise out of his mind as he walked to his parked car in tears. He remembered her fragile body as he gave her that final hug. Parting was hard but there was hope now. Abigail got out of the car and gave him the hug he needed; she always made him feel good and God only knows he needed her strength now more than ever.

After a second or two he spoke. 'Good news, Abi.' George was bursting to tell her about Louise suggesting they move into the house in Camberly Edge, but he didn't know how she'd take it.

'I'm not sure how you'll feel about my news love, but hear me out before you say anything.'

Abigail's smile faltered a little but she listened.

'Daphne, or should I say Louise's house, as you know, is paid for and standing empty. Louise has suggested that we move in and be caretakers, rent free. She's going to give me power of attorney so that I can access the money in the bank too. I explained that we both have jobs and need the income to survive but she said we can use her money until we sort something permanent out. Of course, I told her it would be up to you. It may be that we can get some work in the village. What do you think, love?'

'What about my father, George. He still lives there and he hates us?'

'It's no good anticipating trouble, love. He may even be pleased to see you back, we must have faith.'

'If you think we can do it George we'll give it a try.'

'That's my girl. Anyway it won't be for a while; there are things to sort out first.'

The couple drove home to Birmingham in pensive silence.

Chapter 27

Philip Takes Advantage.

The legal firm of Hopkins & Scott were doing well. New work was plentiful and as soon as one influential client got the right results, others flocked in.

The new receptionist, Deborah Collings, was conscientious from the start and Susannah encouraged and rewarded her hard work and dedication with a salary to match.

The initiative and aptitude of the receptionist was sometimes surprising. She only had to be shown how to do a job once and she rarely made mistakes. Susannah thought it rare to see such a fashionable, beautiful young woman concentrating more on her career than having a good time; but she was grateful. It reminded Susannah a little of herself at that age. The only difference between Susannah and Deborah was that Susannah had her family to support her and Deborah had no-one; she lived alone.

Although polite and courteous Susannah had professional principles which included keeping the staff at arm's length; they were employees and nothing more. Philip was so annoyingly open and friendly to the staff, especially Deborah; it sometimes caused conflict between the couple. Their arguments would always be the same.

'What if she had to be reprimanded, Phil? When you have a friendship with the staff you would find it difficult.' Susannah was getting tired of the same argument.

'I'll just leave all that stuff to you, precious girl. You are so good at it.' His smile and wicked sense of humour mostly annoyed her but also melted her heart. The same argument would come up time after time.

With the workload increasing, it was getting more difficult to get to her parents home during the week. Eva-Lucy was growing fast and Susannah was conscious that she was missing out on all the first things a little one does. The weekends were great, putting Eva-Lucy to bed and being there when she woke up; but week-night visits to see her were growing less frequent. Philip had agreed to do more of the out of hours business work which meant he was staying alone in the city more. Even then Susannah would often be too tired to go home to see her little girl. The more the work came in the harder everything seemed to get.

It was Wednesday afternoon and Susannah wanted to get off from work a little early to make the journey to Kent and her daughter. Deborah took a telephone call at 3pm from the local police station regarding a regular client. He'd been taken into the police station for questioning when they broke down his door at 6 am and entered his flat on a court warrant. The police had found enough cannabis plants growing in his loft to make the whole of London high. He was arrested and later charged. He needed a solicitor present for official questioning.

'You get off, Miss Hopkins. I'll wait for Mr Scott to return from court and explain the details to him. I'm sure he's on his way already.' Deborah always saved the day.

'Thank you Deborah. I'm so looking forward to seeing Eva-Lucy. Thanks again.'

Susannah left the office with her brief case and overnight bag and headed for the tube.

Within minutes of her leaving, Philip walked in with a huge smile on his face that said. 'Look at me, aren't I the clever one.'

'Had a successful day, Mr Scott?' Deborah continued without waiting for a response. 'Mr Scott, you've just missed Miss Hopkins. You have a client at the police station. He was arrested during a police raid. They found cannabis growing in his attic. He wants to speak with you, but the situation looks clear to me. They'll probably keep him overnight and present him to the remand court tomorrow at the magistrate's court. I've checked his file and the antecedents would suggest it will go to Crown and bail is doubtful as he's got several offences of 'fail to appear' and further offences whilst on bail. You can probably keep the police questioning to a minimum by suggesting he pleads guilty for a reduced sentence'

'Well, well! You seem to have picked up a lot of information since you've been here Deborah; very impressive.' Phil gave her one of his 'trying to be sexy' smiles.

'Why don't you come with me, Deb? It's nearly home time and you may learn some more.'

Deborah had her bag and coat in her hand ready to go before he could change his mind. This was just what she was after; some time with Phil, alone.

The police interview was short as Phil knew it would be. His instructions to his clients were always the same; say as little as possible and never be helpful. They were out within the hour.

'I need a drink, Deb. Want to join me?'

'Great,' she responded well to his smile as most women did.

The drink turned into several and Deborah was ready for the night ahead.

'Phil, you can't go back to the flat alone in that state. You need someone to look after you, and, as luck would have it I'm free.'

'Well little Debs,' he put his arm around her small waist. 'That offer suits me just fine. Now how does the saying go? Oh yes, your place or mine?'

'Well mine is closer, maybe not as elegant as yours but on a receptionists pay what do you expect?'

Deborah had Philip Scott just where she wanted him; and she'd wanted him from the first day she'd set eyes on him. If only Susannah could see her now.

The bedsit Deborah had rented was very small. A living room with a small sofa and one armchair, a kitchen in the corner, a pull down bed which she never put back up and a small shower room with the tiniest basin and a loo. There was a small window which had no view apart from a wall but it was neat and tidy. There was a red silk duvet cover with matching pillow cases and after lighting several scented candles around the room it felt warm and cosy.

Philip was oblivious to the décor of the place, he had one thing on his mind and Deborah was pleased to accommodate. In fact, it was frightening how easy Phil found it to betray Susannah; obviously it wasn't the first time. He had little or no conscience.

'Good morning, handsome.'

Deborah stood over the half awake Phil with a mug of freshly ground Columbian coffee. It seemed the beautiful Deborah had a few standards.

'Hey gorgeous, what time is it?'

'Time enough for you to drink your coffee, have a shower and get to the Magistrates court by 9.30. The remand hearings will be starting at 10 o'clock, Boss.'

'I slept like a baby, Debs; and what a great way to wake up.'

'Let's keep last night between us Phil. I can't afford to lose my job.'

'That's fine by me hon, our little secret.'

Philip took a long drink from his mug and raised it into the air.

'Here's to many more nights of love, sweet Deborah Collings.'

Phil hadn't expected that things would go so well last night and staying over at Deborah's certainly wasn't on the cards. The result was he didn't have a clean shirt to wear. Still if that was the price he had to pay for such a great night he was happy and wore his dirty shirt to court for the remand hearing.

He was back at the office by noon and went straight into Susannah's office giving Deborah a sly little wink as he passed.

'How was your morning, love?' he said as he planted a sweet little kiss on her cheek. Absolutely no remorse for his nocturnal actions.

'Eva-Lucy has a cold, I didn't sleep a wink. I think it may go to her chest and she's very hot. Mum is calling the doctor to check her over.'

'You should go back to her, love. Forget work. I'll sort everything out. Our little Eva-Lucy needs her mummy.'

'Are you sure Phil? There's a lot to do!' Susannah was so pleased by his reaction. Maybe he was warming to fatherhood.

'Just go, and ring me when the doctor's been, darling.'

'Thanks, love.' Susannah picked up her bag and coat leaving without a word to Deborah.

Deborah was a little surprised at Susannah quick exit and went into her office where Philip was seated at her desk. She didn't have time to speak.

'We seem to be on again tonight, sexy; Susannah's gone back to Kent.'

'Does that mean we are going steady' Deborah was delighted but laughed as casually as she could.

That is the way things continued. When the cat was away the mice always played.

Philip Scott worked hard and played hard. He was determined to be the best lawyer he could be. It seemed that his duplicity gave him the adrenalin rush he needed to get on top of his game. Managing his lifestyle wasn't easy but he loved every minute of it. Susannah and his child were a small part of his future but he needed them, if only to ensure his success. He needed what the family name of Hopkins would give him; 'Hopkins & Scott – All Law Work Undertaken'. The firm was going far and he wanted the power it offered him. He had thoughts of proposing to Susannah and slowly squeezing her out of the business by having more children. She was a good, devoted mother to Eva-Lucy. Even though she worked, the child was always on her mind. Phil knew her dad wanted her to be a full time mother, so maybe between them he could get his way. In the meanwhile, they needed to build up the practice and Deborah was a gem; she seemed to know exactly what to do and, of course, it was a bonus that she was free with her love.

Over the next couple of months he saw Deborah outside the practice a few times a week and was becoming fond of her. She was younger than Susannah and she allowed him to be in control; he liked being in charge and was even beginning to think long term. Phil was always thinking of the next step, some would say ruthless. If he committed to Susannah he could see himself as the senior partner of the best law firm in London with a subservient wife at home and the choice of many lovers. But there again, he'd have more fun with Deborah. Life was confusing.

The lovers had decided to spend the whole evening at her bedsit rather than eat out; so Deborah offered to cook. Deborah left the office ahead of him with a view to preparing a nice meal. When Philip arrived, there was a lovely smell coming from the two ringed hob. There it was, simmering gently, a saucepan of bolognaise and a pan of pasta next to it. Philip found a cork screw and opened his contribution to the evening; a bottle of Chateauneuf du Pape, leaving it to breathe.

The meal was a slow process and Phil's second bottle came into play. Leaving the dishes, they sat on the small sofa and watched a little television wrapped in each others arms.

'I love you, Philip Scott,' Deborah watched his face closely.

'I do believe I am falling for you too, Miss Collings. How should we celebrate?'

'I'd like to know what we should do about all this love between us, boss.'

The state of play was changing; Deborah was getting a little serious but he hadn't lied. He was falling for her and who could blame him? She was the sweet lover that Phil desired.

'I love you sweet Debs but I have to get more control over the firm; I need to be the senior partner. Otherwise, I'll be back where I started.'

Maybe it was the wine but Deborah liked what he said. It was a side of Phil that Deborah had never seen before. It was a nice side; a vulnerable side and she wanted more.

'What more do you want? We love each other and work well as a team.' She stroked his face.

'No, you don't understand. Susannah is extremely rich and I want, even deserve, some of it.' Phil's expression changed.

'How will you achieve all this Phil?' Deborah probed further.

'I haven't worked it out yet but I know things about Susannah that she would never want to be made public.'

Deborah held his hand gently and guided him to the bed where a night of love awaited.

Around 11 pm Phil's cell phone rang. The couple pulled apart as if they were two naughty children caught doing wrong. They both laughed as Phil got out of bed to get the phone from his jacket pocket. He put his finger to his lips to indicate silence as he could see Susannah's name on his phone. Phil felt a twinge of guilt and worst of all he had to take the call in front of Deborah, there was no where else to go in the small bedsit.

'Hi Darling,' Phil tried to sound casual. 'This is a late call are you all right?'

'Not Really Philip, Where are you?'

There may be a chance that Susannah had come home to the apartment as a surprise so he had to think quickly.

'I'm in my own flat babe; I didn't want to spend the night in our bed without you.' He was beginning to sweat, the excuse was lame.

'It's Eva-Lucy,' Susannah sounded upset, 'It's the cold. It's on her chest and she's very unwell,' Phil could hear the tension in Susannah's voice.

'Do you want me to come straight away?' He felt he had to say it.

'No, I just wanted to talk to you. I'm sure she'll be fine. The doctor's given her some medicine and my mother's here. If there's any change I'll ring.'

Philip put the phone close to his lips and whispered, 'I love you Suzy.'

Susannah was tearful, 'I can't do all this on my own Philip. We have to do something permanent.'

'I know love. We'll talk.'

Deborah was watching his every move as he put his phone back into his jacket pocket.

'What's wrong, Phil?' Deborah ignored the 'I love you' bit.

'It's Eva-Lucy. She has a cold and Susannah is concerned. I'm sure she'll be fine.'

'There's more to your relationship than I know, isn't there Phil? Is Eva your child?'

The look on his face spoke a thousand words.

'Okay Debs, you need to know, you deserve to know. I met Susannah when she joined Benjamin,Scott,Walters & Parsons as a postgraduate looking to do her articles. Her soon-to-be, husband had also joined as a conveyance solicitor. His name was Alex Turner; a Welsh lad from somewhere in Wales I can't pronounce. They were so different Debs, but I suppose that's what attracted them to each other. Susannah only had eyes for Alex.'

'During the time we worked together I showed Susannah the ropes and she observed my court cases. Her career was taking off and she was bypassing me fast. Her dad knew old man Benjamin well so I supposed that helped.'

'Alex and Susannah had a lovely wedding at her parent's home. Their life was perfect until Alex announced that city life was not for him.'

'He'd been brought up on his father's farm in Wales and at that time he wanted more for himself. He qualified as a solicitor and started work as a conveyance lawyer. When he got what he believed he wanted, he realised it wasn't for him so they bought a large house with land, in the back of beyond. A place called Camberley Edge; in Hertfordshire, I think. It was within commuting distance from London, so Susannah travelled every day. Although she insisted that she should keep the London flat for nights when she was on call.'

'Alex was caught up with his new life and Susannah enjoyed city life. She did try to support Alex but their love was stretched to the limits and I'm sorry to say I stepped in. My intentions were almost honourable; by that I mean that I kept her adultery a secret.'

Deborah interrupted. 'Life must have been complicated Phil. I'm not judging you. I'm hardly in a position to do so.'

Philip continued. 'Everyone knows that the Hopkins dynasty is the most financially secure but William Hopkins still holds the reigns. Susannah has inherited his obsession with money but daddy is always the boss. The truth is she wants to make her own fortune and be truly independent. Believe me Debs, William Hopkins is not the kind generous man he portrays; when challenged he's quite the tiger.'

'What about Susannah's mother, Phil? Was she a housewife or did she practice law too?' Deborah asked.

'Mrs Hopkins retired from law when their children were born. Most people forget that Isobel was a top family lawyer herself. She was independent and had a great future when she met William. He put a stop to her career. Susannah told me that she pleaded with William to let her go back to work when the children were grown up and independent. William always gets his way and Susannah has that family trait; she wants to be well-known and rich just like her dad. Her brother, William Jnr is more content with his lot.'

Philip continued and Deborah was content to listen. 'When Alex wanted out of the legal profession it bothered Susannah more than she showed. She had concerns that it may affect her financial situation. Buying a house in the country and retaining the city apartment would obviously slow down her plans for the future, she was torn in two. Alex wasn't expecting any inheritance from his parents as it was made clear to him that his education costs would be all he'd get and his two brothers would share the farm after their father's day. Fortunately for Alex his brothers saw it differently and after selling some of the land off to a housing developer they gave Alex a nice some of money to fund his dream house in the country.'

'It wasn't long before Alex became suspicious of Susannah and me although she always denied everything he had concerns about. After a busy day at the office Susannah decided to go home to Jasmine Cottage one evening without telling Alex. She wanted to surprise him. Her car was at the station at Camberley Edge so after the train journey she drove the short distance home. Parking the car at the front gate she ran up the path and let herself in quietly, hoping to give Alex a pleasant surprise. Well it was she who had the surprise. The noise coming from their bedroom was not what she had expected. Her beloved Alex had another woman in the marital bed. Susannah told me she stood there listening, unable to move or speak for what seemed like ages then turned and ran to her car driving all the way back to the city and into my arms. The couple in her bed never even knew she'd been in the house. I had never seen her so upset, she was devastated, heartbroken but most of all she was angry. I've never seen her like it either before or after. By the following morning she was remarkably calm, but more concerning she had a plan.'

'From that night on Susannah watched every move Alex made. She would take the train and then drive to somewhere near the cottage and park the car out of sight, spending hours watching the house without him knowing. Susannah had become obsessed. When her surveillance revealed nothing she got him away for a weekend break and paid one of her criminal clients to wire the house with sophisticated recording equipment.'

'My God, Phil. That is just so scary; why would she go to all that trouble? If she divorced Alex they would have to split everything which I'm sure would be a good sum of money.'

'Oh come on, Debs. You know Susannah. She would want to take everything from Alex and make him suffer. Some evenings we'd spend together she'd rant and rave that she would see him dead before he got a penny. The next thing I knew Alex was dead and his girlfriend was arrested. So your guess is as good as mine.'

'Do you have the tapes from the recordings she had?'

'As far as I'm aware they are still in the attic of the cottage. She locked it all up when Alex died and I'm sure she's never been back. Maybe from guilt, who knows?'

Philip and Deborah fell asleep in each others arms that night. Philip snoring in complete ignorance and Deborah with a smile of contentment.

Chapter 28

Deborah Reveals All.

Another day at the office for Private Investigator Alan Preston James. The phone rang.

'Al, it's Deb.'

'Hi babe, anything new?'

'Oh yes! Mission accomplished. Last night clinched the deal. Everything is on tape, even Philip Scott's suggestion that Susannah Turner shot her husband. The motive is clear and all we need is to prove she was at the house the night of Alex's demise. I've dismantled the cameras and microphones in the bedsit; we've got him Al, the whole deal is recorded. Anything you come up with now will be supporting evidence.'

'And there's more; she had the cottage in Camberley Edge bugged to get evidence of Alex's adultery with Louise Anderson. It seems that Mrs Turner had a plan. I think my work is done here, Al. Should I come back to Birmingham today? I'm getting a bit edgy being around Susannah Hopkins. She's one clever lady and I don't want to be around if she discovers I've been bedding Philip Scott. This London bedsit is driving me mad too. I feel as if I'm living in a chicken coop. I'm not that keen on the less than desirable Philip Scott either. It was quite an effort to be intimate with him and that's says a lot, considering my history. He's some Casanova, or at least he thinks he is.'

Alan laughed. 'Good work, Miss Collings. Yes you should come home today. Forget handing in your notice; it's best you leave quickly with no trace. I'll deal with the bedsit. I'll cancel the lease with a bit of extra cash to keep them quiet. Text me when you're near Birmingham and I'll meet the train. Oh! Don't forget the tapes, babe, that's the best evidence you could have got.'

Alan rang George Anderson immediately. The plan was coming together and he felt like the cat that got the cream.

'George, it's Alan. Alan James!'

'Alan! Good to hear from you. Any news?' George had been patient; he knew these things take time.

'Certainly have, mate. Maybe enough to start thinking of setting out the case for the Appeal.'

'You don't know how good that sounds Alan. Louise is going under fast. I don't think she'll survive that prison much longer. What do you need me to do?'

'Right now, nothing. We need to meet up in a day or so to go through the information I've collected. The next step is to get a good lawyer to guide us through the procedure.'

'How does Friday suit you Alan? I can be at your office at 10.00 am.'

'Excellent. I wouldn't mention anything to your daughter yet. We don't want to build her hopes up until we've double checked everything.'

'Alright, Alan. See you Friday.'

Alan picked Deborah up from the station at 2.30 p.m. that day and they spent the rest of the afternoon and most of the evening going over every detail. They documented the taped conversations and watched the video recording. The pictures were clear and Philip Scott was easily identifiable. The conversation was written out between Deborah and Philip.

'Can you delete the intimate scenes Al? I'm uncomfortable with them being produced as evidence for all to see.'

The look on Alan's face gave her the answer.

'Good work, Deb. What a perfect honey trap.'

Alan had first met Deborah Collings when he worked as a profiler in the Metropolitan Police Service. He was never directly involved but everyone knew the lovely Deborah Collings. She was making a nice income as a high class call girl and known for it. Unfortunately for the officers involved she was good at evading prosecution. Knowing people in high places got her out of a lot of scrapes.

After her successful life in London, Deborah decided to move back to Birmingham where she had been brought up. She bought an expensive apartment with enough cash for many years.

Alan ran into her in a pub many years after he'd left the Force and set up his business in Birmingham. He had thought about the lovely Deborah through the years. He wondered if she had ever had her comeuppance for all the years she'd evaded the strong arm of the law. Over a few drinks they talked of old times and Deborah was all ears when Alan said she could make good money working for him and staying on the right side of the law for a change. She was becoming bored as a lady of leisure. Her looks and charm were perfect for the jobs Alan was no good at. Deborah was smart and well educated and Alan often wondered why such a gorgeous girl would use herself as a prostitute, even high class. The partnership worked well and their caseload was expanding which meant they were also earning a lot of money.

This case, in particular, was more complicated and they had to get real evidence that would stand up in court to get Louise out of prison. Appeals are never easy and they'd only get one crack at it.

Alan wanted desperately to get his hands on the tapes that were, apparently, still in the loft of Jasmine Cottage. It had to be done legally in order to present it as evidence, but Susannah could not know about it. The case had to be watertight and flawless to stand any chance of winning the appeal.

Deborah had been told by Philip that Susannah had not or could not go back to the cottage. The dogs had been sold and the cottage locked up by her brother. Even after the birth of her child she had put Camberley Edge right out of her mind not even considering selling the cottage. It was almost as if she couldn't face returning to the scene of the crime. The fact that Louise was imprisoned for Alex's murder made it easier on Susannah; there was no immediate urgency to deal with the cottage. In Susannah's twisted mind she probably thought it was divine intervention that Louise would suffer, not for the murder but for the much more serious offence of getting one over on Susannah Turner by bedding her husband.

It was Friday, 10 am and George was seated opposite Alan James at his office in town.

'George, I have a recording of Philip Scott speaking with a young woman whom I planted in the office of Hopkins & Scott in London. It seems that Phil is a bit of a player, as I suspected. The woman is someone I met when I was in the Police Force and she got a job with their firm as a receptionist. She built up a good relationship with Phil over the past few months, although getting close to Susannah was impossible. It soon became apparent that Phil was the one who would give her the information we needed, of course he was oblivious to the set up. He showed an interest in Deborah since the first day. Please don't judge her but Deborah Collings used to be a high class call girl; so high class she was virtually untouchable by the law. We met several years later and now I often use her for jobs that need a honey trap. I pay through the nose for her services but she takes far less time to get the information I need than if I worked alone.'

'That sounds perfectly good to me. I'm certainly not in a position to judge others.'

Alan continued. 'The thing is George, knowing someone is guilty and proving it is very different. We could be trying to get the right sort of evidence against Susannah for years without Debs and her special expertise at getting what she wants from men. She's also a very bright, well educated person and had no problem getting herself the job at the firm of solicitors.'

'So as it stands I have this recording of Philip telling Debs that Susannah knew all about Alex's affair with Louise. She had the cottage in Camberley Edge bugged by professional criminals and according to Phil, all the recordings are still in the loft, untouched.'

'Is all this enough to put Susannah in the frame, Alan?'

'Maybe, but I would like to place Susannah in the area of Jasmine Cottage by another means just to clinch it. Susannah was questioned by the police at the time of Alex's murder and she said on record that she was in London at that time. I have a few contacts still on the force and I've called in a few favours.

They're checking CCTV footage at garages, shops etc. on that night. They'll come back to me if they find something.'

'If what Deborah got Philip to say is true then it adds up to our belief that Susannah killed Alex, but it's only that, a belief.' George understood.

'You're right George, but it casts a doubt on Louise's conviction. Having said that, I want to find something more solid that will give us the evidence to get the case re-opened. Susannah is a clever woman and if we go in with what we have, she may bluff her way out of it. Not only is she a good lawyer, she has nerves of steel to have done a thing like this. We just need to put her in the area of Camberley Edge on that night; it will swing the case and prove she is not only a liar but a killer too.'

'I can't thank you enough Alan, you're doing a great job.'

The men shook hands then George left for home.

Later that day Alan had a telephone call from his friend in the Force.

'Hey, Al my old friend. How are you, buddy?'

'Good Mick. Are you ringing with some good news?'

'I certainly am. There was CCTV footage of Susannah Turner at a petrol station near Camberley Edge. When she filled the car up the silly girl paid with her credit card, can you believe that of her? Susannah Turner doesn't know just how dammed good we all are Al. I've copied it all and I'll email it to you today.'

'I think her overconfidence will cause her downfall. Thanks Mick, I'm grateful.'

'No problem Al. It's good to be in touch with you after all these years. Any time. Remember that mate!'

'Well that's it, the final piece of the puzzle. Now we're ready to roll.' Alan said out loud as he punched the air with satisfaction.

The next step was to find a good lawyer who will be able to manage such a case. Alan spent time ringing a few he knew in the Birmingham area and found out something interesting. A man named Joseph Golding had graduated with Susannah and worked for some time as a criminal lawyer in London. It seemed that their friendship had been pushed to one side for the sake of competition. The strength of the Hopkins Dynasty almost suffocated Joseph to the point that, as bad feelings go, theirs was the worst. Joe was good and an obvious threat. He despised Susannah for allowing this to happen; if he had been weaker it could have ruined his career. Joe believed that Susannah's future in the legal profession was more important to her than any other thing or any one.

More importantly, years ago Joe and Susannah spent a drunken night together and she had confided in him that there was a clause to her inheritance. William Hopkins was a tough husband and father and believed his daughter needed to be controlled; to be kept in line and respectable for the sake of the family name. The clause was simple; divorce and you lose everything.

Alan couldn't believe his ears. That gave her a clear motive. The reasons behind the threat are unimportant. All they needed to prove was that Susannah believed it.

Alan Preston James P.I. was known never to take his work home with him; a clear and simple rule. On this occasion, he broke his own rule. The facts and information that he needed were now all in place and he just couldn't stop himself from smiling. The evidence against 'The Wicked Witch of Camberley Edge' and her almost successful plot to get away with murder was now a watertight case. To put Susannah Turner behind bars and free the innocent Louise Anderson was the biggest case he'd ever had. He was one proud P. I.

That night Alan worked on case-managing the whole project. In his years on the Force he knew how important the presentation of evidence would be. The Court of Appeal would not consider a case badly presented. He had to make sure it was perfect. The conversation he'd had with Joe Golding made him realise that he would make a better witness than advocate to the barrister. His relationship with Susannah was crucial so another criminal lawyer was secured and Joe became a witness, even if only on paper and by means of a written section 9 statement.

It was almost midnight but Alan wanted to ring George. George and Abigail were watching a late film but when the telephone rang he knew it would be Alan.

'I've done it George. I can place Susannah at a petrol station just outside Camberley Edge on the night that Alex was shot.'

'Oh my God! I can't believe it.'

'There's more George. There was a clause in William Hopkin's will that if Susannah divorced then she would not inherit her share of his fortune. That gives her a clear motive to kill Alex rather than divorce him.'

'Why would her father do that Alan? I don't understand.'

'That really doesn't matter, George. We can order that a copy of the will be examined for confirmation. If that fails then my source will testify. His name is Joseph Golding and he was once a friend of Susannah through University and also in London as a practitioner. Apparently there's bad blood between them now and he's prepared to help.'

'I've found a good lawyer that will, if appointed, check my notes and file for an Appeal. I don't foresee any problems from here on in, the evidence is safe.'

'I can't thank you enough Alan; you've made an old man very happy.' They both laughed.

George was elated and couldn't wait to see his Louise. George was seated before Louise was brought in, which was unusual. When she appeared in the doorway George could see why. Not only was she her usual pale self but she found it hard to walk without the help of one of the guards. As she came closer George could see she had bruises and cuts to her face.

'What on earth has happened to you? Who has done this to you?'

'Don't, dad! I had a fall.'

'I don't think that's the result of a fall, I want to know the truth. They won't get away with this.' George was so angry.

'Listen dad, if you say something it will get back to the wing and make it worse for me. It's been dealt with. Please dad!'

'Are you in any danger?'

'No, not now. Do you remember me mentioning Tracy, my cell mate?'

'Yes love.' George reached out to hold her hand.

'Well, she's been moved to another secure wing where she is confined to her cell twenty three hours each day so I'm on my own for a while. Tracy loses her temper a lot and there's not much I could have done. The screws...'

'Don't say that love. You mean the guards. Criminals call them screws and you're not a criminal.'

'Yes, the guards. They don't like it when there's fighting so I told them I fell off my bunk. They knew the truth though, because they moved her out immediately. She's sick dad, sick in her mind.'

George held her hand tightly; his precious girl had learned to survive this awful place. Now he knew he had to get her out soon.

'I've got good news darling! We have enough evidence for an appeal; it's just a matter of time now.'

'How long, dad?'

'We must be patient a little longer; not too long.' He had to give her hope.

Dad? I want you to move into the house as soon as you can and when I'm out of this place I want us all to live together. You, me and Abigail.'

A tear fell from George's eye and he squeezed his lovely daughter's hand. He didn't say anything, there was no need.

Chapter 29

George Moves Back to Camberley Edge.

The lawyer Alan wanted to appoint for the appeal was expensive but an experienced practitioner who had represented many appellants over the years and was rarely unsuccessful. He had not only an expertise in these matters but a reputation above all others for his simple honesty. This had gained him respect over the years, in all areas of the judiciary. Both Alan and George thought it wiser to employ a professional to manage the case from now on; it was important to get it right from the start. To lose at this stage would be catastrophic. It would be difficult to obtain leave to appeal second time around if the first one had been rejected

Gerald Samuel had come up through the ranks of his profession. The first of his family to chose an academic career and, coincidentally, he originally came from Wales just like Alex.

Alan and George decided to meet him together the first time. Alan would lay out the facts of the evidence and George was there for the emotional angle, just in case Mr Samuel rejected the job.

He didn't. His interest was obvious from the start and Alan knew they had him. Gerald Samuel wasn't cheap but he was good.

'I'll need to have sight of William Hopkins' will and a warrant of access for the police to retrieve any evidence there may be at Jasmine Cottage. With a bit of luck the bugging equipment will still be there. In itself, the fact that Susannah Turner wanted evidence to corroborate any sordid allegiance between her husband and Louise to be true is inconclusive. However, it certainly creates a picture of the character of the, soon to be, defendant.' George couldn't help showing his relief and was impressed that Mr Samuel was working on his action plan already.

Mr Samuel continued.

'Leave all that to me Mr James; I can get that sorted out. I must say, sir, you have done quite a remarkable job in getting all this evidence. It leaves little doubt that Louise Anderson is most certainly as innocent of this matter as Susannah Turner is guilty.' Alan smiled in gratitude for the praise.

'It seems to me, gentlemen that we have excellent grounds for the case to be reopened and I am very hopeful that leave for the appeal will be granted. I will prepare the papers immediately and I believe it would be appropriate, in this case, to go directly to the Royal Courts of Justice Appeal Court, Criminal Division. You probably know that the primary hearing will be by a single justice who will make a decision as to whether or not the case is strong enough to be heard by a full bench.'

Most of what was said went over George's head, but Alan seemed to understand what he was saying. Just like Alex, Mr Samuel came from a long line of hill farmers but his upbringing was not apparent in his manner or in the way he spoke. There was no doubt that he was definitely the man for the job. He knew the procedure and how to avoid irrelevant, bureaucratic delays, which impede the desired results.

The men shook hands before Alan and George left. Outside the office the two men hugged and George shed a tear of relief.

'Well, George! I believe we've done it. After all this time we can now relax and all we have to do is wait for the result. It's looking good.'

Things didn't move as quickly as George would have liked; but that's typical of legal proceedings. He had to be patient; there was nothing else to do.

Abigail was his strength through all this and continued to support him in every way. She knew he was anxious about the appeal hearing and tried to take his mind off it as far as she could.

'I think it's time we moved into Louise's house and get things ready for her homecoming, George.'

'You're right love. I'll terminate the rental contract on this place and we'll move soon.'

The flat they were renting had been furnished when they moved in. They bought small items to make it a home but it wouldn't take much effort to move.

Within two weeks they were on their way. The move would be more difficult for Abigail. She hadn't had contact with her dad for years, although she had written, sent birthday and Christmas cards. To live a few streets away and be ignored would be hard for both her and George. They knew they'd done wrong and were prepared for name calling but together they would somehow make a good life for themselves in Camberley Edge. They had to be strong for one and other.

The house looked lovely from the outside and the pair sat in the car for a while admiring their new home.

'Come on, love! I expect there's work to be done inside. We can't sit here for ever.' George was excited to be back in Camberley Edge, but he had a few reservations. He hoped that Madge had spread the word to the people he knew about them returning to the village so that it wouldn't be a shock to them when they met in the street.

George opened the front door and pick up a pile of mail before he walked through to the lounge with Abigail following. It didn't smell too good inside; there had been no fresh air for some time and it seemed that there were several families of spiders squatting. After moving their belongings in, Abigail checked to see if there was bedding in the airing cupboard. There was, but it smelled dreadful so she closed the airing cupboard door quickly, making a mental note that it had to be dealt with within the next few days.

'We'll have to manage with the car rugs for tonight George and I'll go shopping for new bedding tomorrow.'

'Okay, love! Whatever you say.'

The bedding belonged to the landlord at the flat and they had, therefore, left it behind. Abigail brought all their cleaning materials from the kitchen, she felt a bit mean as the landlord had stocked the cupboards when they moved in. On reflection, it was a small gesture considering, the cost of the rent.

George found a vacuum cleaner under the stairs and started getting the dust off the furniture and curtains whilst Abigail washed all the carpetless floors. It started to smell a little better and soon it looked good. The spiders which stayed to watch were probably sucked up into the nozzle of the cleaner. If they hadn't had the sense to take cover in all the nooks and crannies available to them.

The house wasn't big as far as room sizes were concerned but it had clearly been cared for. Each room was nicely decorated and the furniture was expensively classical. The floors were the original wood and there were several rugs scattered around the downstairs rooms for effect. George loved the big open fireplace in the lounge,| but he saw the house through Abigail's eyes and knew it wasn't her style at all. It was a typical village cottage with low ceilings and small windows but with an unusually large garden, a corner house with trees all around giving privacy.

From the kitchen window they could see the flower garden was overgrown and the two greenhouses were in a state. The glass was green with mildew and you couldn't see a thing inside. George knew there would have been beautiful plants and flowers inside when Daphne was alive. She cared for her plants almost as well as she cared for Louise. He was sad that they had all been left to rot.

Over a cup of coffee the newly installed couple chatted about strategy and agreed that the garden would be left until the house was brought up to scratch and that would take time. Abigail wanted to paint the whole house to get rid of that damp, dusty smell. George made a managerial decision that that would be Abigail's task for the coming week.

It took a week to get the house in good shape as far as the cleaning was concerned. Everywhere was so dusty. There was even dust inside the kitchen cabinets; Daphne would have been heart broken at the state of her lovely cottage.

As time went on it began to look like home but Abigail wanted a few things of her own. She broached the subject when she thought George was in a good mood.

'Please love,' she stopped and took his hand in hers, 'If it's alright with you I'd like to buy a new bed. It doesn't have to be expensive but I don't want to sleep on Daphne's for ever. I think some new curtains would look nice too. Daphne's are lovely but I would like lighter, prettier ones and it would make the room more airy.'

George couldn't resist the request and, once again, work began.

When the telephone rang one evening George answered it.

'I heard you were back in the village, George Anderson.'

George knew immediately who the caller was.

'Mr Flint. How are you?'

'Bloody angry.'

'It's been a while. Can we sort this all out?'

'Why do you think I'm ringing, vicar? Oh no you're not the vicar any more are you? You're a two timing rat. It's not you I want to talk to; it's my daughter.'

Abigail had realised that the caller was her dad and took the phone off George.

'Dad?'

'Yes, Abi. It's me. I was told you were back in Camberley Edge.'

'Can I come around to see you dad?'

'That's why I'm ringing. Come around tomorrow morning.'

The telephone went dead.

'George, he wants to see me.'

'I'm so pleased for you darling. When are you going?'

'Tomorrow morning.'

Abigail slept well that night. The call from her dad was such good news. George had said things would work out and they are. She was sure she could convince her father to see George too, but maybe not just yet.

197

Up early, showered and best dress; Abigail was ready to see her father.'

His welcome was cool, but it was early days yet. They drank tea together and Abigail was full of expectation. It was looking good.

'I didn't think you'd see me after I've ignored you for so long Abi.'

'Don't be silly dad as long as we're together now, that's all that matters.'

'I hated that man for so long; he took you from me.'

'George is a good man dad. We love each other and we're happy.'

'What does he say about me?'

'Nothing, just that he wants to put things right; for my sake. Is that possible, dad?'

'Maybe we can start again, slowly.'

Edward Flint was not the man he was. In the time Abigail had been away he'd grown old. The house was not as well cared for and he seemed lost; without a purpose.

Knowing it was time for forgiveness, Edward was prepared to make amends.

When Abigail left her family home that day she was elated and hopeful. Excitedly relating every word that had been said between her and her dad to George before even taking off her coat.

The door bell rang. Not expecting a caller, George responded.

He paled when he saw who was standing there.

'George! I said that I wanted to put the past behind me and I could see the relief in Abigail face. I don't want to hurt my daughter any more than I already have.'

'Come in, Ed.'

George opened the door wide as Edward Flint walked passed him. Any one could see this was a difficult moment for both men but they had one thing in common, Abigail; the woman they both loved. For that reason emotions were high, but not with anger. That was all behind them now.

Chapter 30

The Appeal.

The day had arrived. The preliminary hearing by a single justice had been successful in that the rules prescribed the form and content of the Notice and Grounds of Appeal and were of an acceptable standard thereby the Leave of Appeal had been granted. The evidence was considered sufficient for a second hearing conducted by two High Court Judges and Lord of Justice Appeal Judge sitting together as a Bench.

The Royal Courts of Justice simply called the Law Courts in London is a magnificent building which houses both the High Court and the Court of Appeal of England and Wales. The elaborate entrance hall was more than a little intimidating to those who were unfamiliar with it and Alan had wished he'd taken George there beforehand. The large, high ceilings of the wide Main Hall are breathtaking for first time visitors. Gothic arches leading off the hall with exquisite flooring. The building is located in the Borough of Westminster and opened in 1882 it was designed and built by George Edmund Street in the architectural style of Gothic Revival.

Alan and George arrived early and were directed to the higher level of the building where their courtroom for the case was situated. There were rows and rows of closed doors on one side and an open landing area on the other side overlooking that enormous entrance hall. When they found their courtroom they were told to sit in the spectator's gallery. The gallery had its own entrance because of its situation within the courtroom. It was like sitting in the circle of a theatre and they looked down over the body of the court but the Bench was almost at the same level and they were immediately opposite. The practitioners of the court hadn't come in yet, so George and Alan sat and chatted quietly. Abigail had decided that she would stay home and prepare a meal for later. George realised that she was nervous so didn't push her to attend with him.

'Will Louise be sitting near us, Alan?' George asked nervously.

'Oh no. She will be in the dock.' Alan pointed to the dock.

'I see,' said George. 'This is all so new to me.'

'Don't worry George. If you don't understand anything just ask.'

Before George could thank Alan for his patience the gallery door opened to their right and Mr and Mrs Turner walked in, Alex's mother and father. George nodded to them not knowing who they were and they sat behind. The seats in the gallery slowly filled. Bob and Madge, Edward Flint and other familiar faces from the village. George felt anxious. There was movement in the body of the court, the practitioners were arriving.

Gerald Samuel worked with the barrister who was presenting Louise's appeal and he sat behind him in the court room to give help and advice on facts that may crop up unexpectedly.

There was lots of chattering going on until a court officer stood to his feet.

'All rise'. He spoke loudly. Everyone got to their feet as the three judges entered from a rear entrance and walked in line to their seats on the Bench. Before taking their seats they bowed in time and received a reciprocal bow from the court practitioners.

The case was read and the appellant was invited to stand to be identified. Louise looked frail. Her already pale complexion stood out against the red of her hair and she gripped the wooden barrier before her, as she told the court her name. George could see she was tearful and her body trembled as she stood, so scared, before those who would decide on her future. George feared for his daughter's life if this appeal should fail.

Reasons for and against the case were heard. The barrister leading the appeal stated his case eloquently and with the precision needed to convince the decision makers that the law was not only wrong in the conviction of this young girl but of the gross lack of research by the team of investigators into the prima face information which should have resulted in the real perpetrator being imprisoned.

Evidence was placed before the Bench; petrol receipts, cctv footage was shown, evidence collected by the talented Deborah Collings. The appellants team had been granted that evidence relating to character of Susannah Hopkins should be admissible and Joseph Golding, Susannah's ex-colleague, was called and spoke with conviction against her as would be expected of such and experienced lawyer and someone who clearly despised the woman for her callousness and mindful deceit.

The recording evidence that had been rescued from Jasmine Cottage was not clear and the mechanics of the instruments had failed soon after installation so not as reliable as originally supposed.

Madge rang George one evening and told him to be prepared. Even more villagers had decided to attend court for the decision. Whether out of a morbid curiosity or maybe out of concern that Louise had really been misjudged. Whatever the reason, George was more than happy for the truth to be known.

Shan and Bryn Turner were staying in a hotel near the Court House and attended every day. They were surprised to see the sudden interest by Camberley Edge villagers. George felt his daughter's pain and embarrassment as the details of her affair with a married man, Alex Turner, was discussed in open court. George felt it showed her naivety, typical of a young girl with no experience of life. It also showed that although she was compliant; the affair was guided by Alex himself; for whatever reason. Most of all it showed her love and commitment to Alex Turner which put in question her ability to kill the man she loved.

When the decision was being made the court room was emptied. The observers gathered in the large reception hall at the centre of the building. Louise had been taken to the court cells and George worried for her; she was so vulnerable and now she was alone.

Abigail had come with George for the decision; she and George sat in a corner of the reception hall with Alan James. They were exhausted after the stress of the case and the slowness of the procedure. Alan was convinced that they had done everything within their powers to overthrow the decision of the first trial court but George was scared. Scared to believe that this could be the end of their nightmare. Scared to even contemplate going home without Louise. Abigail took his hand, sharing his pain.

Bryn and Shan Turner walked over to the couple introduced themselves and asked if they could have a word.

'Of course George whispered.'

'Whatever happens today, we know that Louise is innocent of killing our Alex.' Bryn spoke slowly and carefully.

'If God is with us today then Louise will walk free and live the rest of her life as she should. Shan and I have suffered because we believed that Lucy-Eva was our granddaughter and Susannah was obstructive when we wanted to see her. Now we know the truth; she carried the burden of lies and guilt which you have revealed to us. How you've managed to uncover all this deception I can't imagine; it must have not only cost you a fortune but unbelievable determination. I'd like to shake your hand, Sir!'

George stood and shook the hand of Bryn Turner. There wasn't an onlooker with a dry eye.

It seemed like hours until the court usher's voice rang out calling everyone back to the courtroom.

'This is it Abi. I'm shaking.' George was pale.

It took a while for the observers to settle back into their seats. George's eyes were firmly fixed on the dock. The door inside the dock opened and Louise took her seat. Her small frame only filled only half of her chair. Her eyes were red from crying.

'If you just do one thing for me God; please let it be today. Let me hold my daughter as a free woman.' George whispered.

'All stand!' The usher called and the court was complete.

Everyone but for Louise and her keepers sat, and the decision was announced. It wasn't easy to understand as a lay person and it took so long. George just wanted to hear the words. 'You are free to go.'

That didn't happen and George was getting even more scared.

The pronouncement seemed long and drawn out to the listeners in the observation gallery. The Lord Justice of the Appeal was speaking. He gave no clue as to the decision of the Bench. Then the words that everyone needed to hear came.

'Miss Turner we find in favour of the appeal and you are free to leave the courtroom and enjoy your life as a free woman.'

Those exact words told George that his prayers had been heard. The people in the viewing gallery stood and applauded as Louise was released from the dock and into the arms of her father.

Justice had been done.

All George wanted was to get home but that was too much to ask. There were reporters waiting outside; George drew his last ounce of energy from deep within and stood tall as he spoke loud and clear.

'It has taken a long time. It has been so emotionally hard to bear. We've come to the end of the road but with a good result. Today we've all seen that there is justice and I am so proud of my daughter Louise. I would like to thank Mr and Mrs Turner for their kind words today. The people from Camberley Edge who have come to learn the truth. A man who has become my friend and without whom none of this would have happened; Mr Alan Preston James Private Investigator. Last but certainly not least I would like to thank my partner, Abigail, for her love and support. Now I just want to take my girls home.'

Coming from the back of the crowd George could hear Alan calling his name.

'George, wait a second. They've just arrested Susannah. I believe the police were called and she must have been detained after her evidence.'

'Oh my God! What a perfect day, Alan.'

'Take Louise home and we'll talk in a few day George.'
They shook each others hand, both feeling the friendship that
had grown between them. George held the hands of the two
women he loved above all else.

'I wish mum was here to see this, dad.'

'She knows darling. She's watching.'

The journey home was long and quiet. They pulled up in
front of the house and Louise gave a huge sigh of relief. She was
so weak and exhausted she found it impossible to get out of the
car. Abigail took her arm and helped the frail Louise as they
walked down the path together with George running ahead to
open the door. Inside she fell against her father and sobbed.
They all stood together in the hall crying, laughing and clinging
to each other.

Abigail helped Louise to her newly decorated bedroom.

'Take a short nap, Lou; build up your strength. Then I'll
sort out something for tea.'

Louise lay on top of her pink duvet and sunk into the
soft, fluffy pillows.

'You don't know how good this feels after prison
blankets.'

They laughed together.

'I'm sorry for everything Abigail; you've really been so
good to me and especially supporting my dad.'

Abigail held Louise's hand for a minute, and then left
her to sleep.

When Abigail went into the lounge, George was sitting
reading some cards that had been put through the letterbox.

'What have you got there, love?'

'Cards from well-wishers in the village who seem to
want to make amends. I think we should accept graciously and
put the past behind us.'

'I agree. Now what shall we have for tea?'

There was a knock at the front door.

Abigail ran to answer it. It was Madge with a casserole
dish in her hands.

'Hello, Abigail! How are you, dear?'

'I'm well thank you Madge. Please come in! I'm afraid Louise is taking a nap.'

'Oh that's fine. I've brought you a lamb casserole just in case you hadn't thought about dinner tonight.' Madge put the dish onto a rack on the kitchen unit.

'I hadn't, to be honest. Thank you so much. It smells delicious; will you stay and share it with us Madge?'

'Thank you, but I think you need time as a family. How is Louise?'

'She's really exhausted, I don't know how she's made it this far. Prison life is very difficult and some of the women on her wing were less than friendly. George and I will keep a close eye on her; I wouldn't be surprised if she needs specialist help to get over the ordeal.'

'I'm so sorry, Abigail, for everything. I can't begin to understand what you've all been through but this is a new beginning for you as a family. If there's anything I can do, you only have to ask.'

'There is one thing, Madge. When Louise is back on her feet she'll need something to keep her busy. Would you have enough work at the post office to give her a job; part time would be great.'

'I certainly will need some help and Louise would be ideal. Just let me know when.'

'I will Madge. Thank you very much!'

'Enjoy the meal!' Madge smiled as she left.

Abigail was proud of herself. A job would be good for Louise, when she's ready.

George shouted his thanks from the lounge.

'I'll pop into the shop to see you tomorrow, Madge.'

'Alright, George.'

Things were going well for them all. Louise started working for Madge. Abigail applied for a job as a trainee teaching assistant at the village school and was accepted; she also spent time at her father's house and he at hers.

George, Abigail and Louise were sitting at the breakfast table one morning and Abigail sensed George was a little quieter than usual.

'What's the matter, love?'

Oh, nothing really. I just feel that I'd like to get a job but I don't know where to start.'

'I think you should relax and let us take care of you for a while. What do you think Lou?'

'I think Abi's right, dad. You need to take things easy until you feel ready. Anyway, there are still some jobs to do around here.' Louise gestured to the garden.

'Alright! I'll start on the greenhouses first. You can't even see through the windows they're so dirty with overgrown and dead plants. Then when they are cleared I may turn over some of the garden to plant some vegetables. I quite fancy myself as 'what d'you call it?' I know 'self sufficient'.'

The girls laughed, but they both agreed it was a good idea.

'I've been thinking, dad. When I was in 'that place' I started a course with the Open University. I love working with Madge but I thought I might use some of mum's money for university. What do you think?'

'I think that would be just what mum would have wanted for you darling. I'll get some information off the internet.

George's smile showed how much he loved his daughter the lawyer to be. He was so proud.

George was sitting alone at the breakfast table the following morning. Louise and Abigail had left for work and he was trying to build up the enthusiasm he needed to sort out the greenhouses. He was writing a plan of attack as was his usual way of starting new projects. The telephone rang and Alan James was on the other end.

'Alan,' said George cheerily. 'Has the cheque bounced?'

'Not at all George. Your money is safely in my bank account. I'm ringing to let you know that Susannah Turner was sentenced yesterday. I'm delighted to tell you that the judge in the case showed little or no mercy. The pronouncement was long and drawn-out but he basically said that she was guilty of planning the murder callously and covering her tracks with a false alibi. Lying under oath and allowing an innocent young girl to be punished for a crime she hadn't committed.'

'How long did she get, Alan?'

'A life sentence with a minimum of thirty-five years inside. She deserves every minute of it, George. This is all down to you, my friend.'

Alan had also found out that Philip Scott was not proved to be involved in any way, but was happy to legally sign over his and Susannah's daughter, Eva-Lucy, to William and Isobel Hopkins's care and ultimate adoption in return for the business. Of course, he'll need a new receptionist.

George felt relieved that it was all over but glad to put the whole matter behind them and get on with their lives. George gave his sincere thanks to Alan without whom none of this would have happened and Louise would still be behind bars. They said their goodbyes for the last time.

That night a large bottle of champagne was opened to celebrate the news and George announced that on Monday morning at 9 am he would commence his duties as greenhouse clearer. They laughed together and enjoyed the evening with nothing more on their mind than being a family and celebrating their future.

Chapter 31

Cleaning the Greenhouses.

Monday morning came around and George was ready and eager to fulfil his promise and get started on clearing the green-houses. He had always been an early riser and since Abigail and Louise had become the bread winners of the family, George had taken it upon himself to make them each a packed lunch for work every day. After a hearty breakfast they were on their way and George planned to enjoy his third cup of strong tea alone before starting his chores. The daily paper fell onto the mat just as he sat at the kitchen table to drink his tea. With absolutely no will-power at all he thought it would do no harm to take a few minutes extra and scan the headlines.

A few minutes turned into half an hour and George shook himself into action. He cleared away the breakfast dishes and went looking for the heavy duty gardening gloves Abigail had bought for the job ahead. She had also bought a mask to prevent him inhaling any nasty smells or even gases that could still be lurking amongst the pots of dead orchids. Now, wearing the appropriate clothing and protective gear, George was ready for action and the task ahead. The decision had been made that everything should be put in large heavy duty plastic bags and taken to the nearby farm to be used, in time to come, as compost. The farmer was grateful and George was glad to get rid of it all in one go.

George took the keys off the hook in the kitchen and went outside. He had decided to remove the greenhouse door completely so that he had enough space to take a wheel barrow inside. Easier said than done, but after about an hour the door was off the first greenhouse and work began. The air was rancid and George tried to open a window that appeared to be stuck fast.

The first green house to be emptied was the largest and contained hundreds of small orchids that had perished. They did, in fact, smell quite considerably, so George was glad of the mask. It took most of the morning to clear that one alone. The work was strenuous and not familiar to George; every part of him ached, so he decided to take a break. When making the girls packed- lunches, he'd made an extra sandwich for himself, so with the help of yet another cup of tea George relaxed for thirty minutes.

Back to work with one more greenhouse to clear. George could see it contained some of the more developed orchids which had been ready for sale. Even though they were dead and had fallen over with the weight of the plant overcoming the dry earth in the pot, it was clear that they had at one time been quite beautiful.

George never thought for one moment that this scene would make him so emotional but his eyes filled with tears. He remembered his late wife's love of these wonderful plants and how she must have worked so hard to develop her business, making it profitable enough to give her and Louise a good life. He found an old stool in the corner and sat for a while thinking of Daphne. She must have felt so hurt the day he had told her he was leaving the village with Abigail. George remembered the parlour in the vicarage with all the shelves full of books and the deep-piled red carpet that Daphne vacuumed daily. He sadly recalled the look of surprise on her face. She didn't have a clue about his affair, his other life. How it all must have broken her heart. George carried so much guilt.

He remembered her as a young girl, so beautiful it took his breath away. Her lovely fair, wavy hair. Her hourglass figure that he knew other young men admired but he also knew she only had eyes for him and he enjoyed the security in knowing that. He never once doubted her love for him and truly believed they would be together forever.

George imagined her horror when Louise was arrested. Daphne must have fallen apart; she blamed herself for Alex's death and even said it was she that was totally to blame, not her beloved daughter. Madge had told him that she had no alternative other than to call the doctor in to see Daphne. His

beloved Daphne had been tranquilised to the point that she
didn't know or understand what was going on. George was
grateful to Madge for all she'd done to help her friend.

He touched the dead leaves and flowers of what had
once been a black orchid and remembered Daphne correcting
him. 'It's not black its dark purple.' But it always looked black
to George. He began to feel close to Daphne, here in her greenhouse with all her orchids, even though they were dead. He
smiled as he thought of Daphne surrounded by such beautiful
orchids. These flowers must have been so lovely once. He
imagined her tending to them each day and being so proud when
she presented them at the village flower festival; she must have
grown and sold hundreds and hundreds to have made so much
money.

Looking upwards he spoke softly.

'What were you thinking Daph? Why kill yourself,
leaving Louise alone. Why? You were always the best mother to
our girl. Why leave her when she needed you most? Why didn't
you even go to court? It's just not like you to have behaved like
that.'

'There's work to be done,' he said out loud, trying to
pull himself together. He got a black sack and started putting the
dead plants into it one by one and shelf by shelf. The plants
were loose in their pots through lack of water so they came out
easily. George got into a rhythm of pulling the plant and
throwing it into the waiting plastic bag; one after another. As he
continued down the line of pots an envelope fell from between
them and onto the floor of the green house where the earth that
had missed the bags had settled.

George took off his mask as he picked up the dirty
envelope. He looked at the handwriting. It was Daphne's. He
removed his gloves and stood staring for what seemed a long
time just looking at the envelope not knowing quite what to do.
It was addressed to Madge and the correct thing to do would be
to give it to her. Instead, he put it into his jacket pocket and
walked back into house.

George needed time to think. Should he open the letter? Should he give it to Madge? It was addressed to her after all. He needed time. He needed a cup of strong tea. After filling the empty kettle and putting it on he sat at the kitchen table. He'd feel better after a nice cup of tea, he thought. At least, that was what he had always told his parishioners when they had a problem. The kettle boiled and knocked itself off. George poured the steaming water over the tea bag and waited. His mind was dancing from one question to another.

Surely he had the right to read this letter; it was from Daphne after all.

There again it was addressed to Madge, but she wouldn't mind. Would she?

He sat, with his tea, at the kitchen table and placed the envelope in front of him. He listened to the tick of the wall clock as it broke his silence. His tea was half drunk when he ripped open the letter and began to read.................

The Letter.

My dearest friend Madge,

I'm sitting here at my kitchen table trying to make

sense of what I'm about to do. Sense is not something

I have been accustomed to recently. My sense has been

taken from me by the mind altering pills I've taken with

the hope of finding a way forward and out of this

dreadful state. I have struggled and suffered more than any soul should do and I can see no alternative but to end my life and free myself from this agony.

I cannot go on with this ache inside that never leaves me and the heartache that never ends. I'm living in a dream. No, a nightmare.

It will end tonight.

This letter and my deeds will transport me beyond this ignorant present, and I feel a future in that instant. Whether it be with my God or in purgatory where some, when they know the truth, may say I should be.

Where do I start? Madge, my life long friend. You've always been there for me.

To thank you for being my friend seems inadequate but you have been the only one that truly understood how I felt as I

sank into the depths of despair, the only real friend that would listen, always. You sat with me when I needed someone. You were that someone that I could open my heart to in the months after George left us. I'm sure it's fair to say my life ended that day and although my body lived on I knew my heart and mind were simply going through the motions of being alive. You understood that, dearest Madge.

Then there's Alex Turner, oh how I hated that man. I had become trapped by my own deceit to keep his dirty secret. He stole my little girl's heart and broke it before my eyes. There was no question in my mind Madge; he had to pay. It was so clear at the time that I had to do something, yet afterwards nothing was clear and would never be clear again, if the doctors had their way. Today, my friend, everything is clear and I have to act quickly before the mist surrounds me again. Oh how my bones ache!

When they took my precious girl away, I never dreamt that it would end like this. I begged them to listen to me; I told them my Louise was innocent. You know Louise as well as I do, how could they believe her capable of murder? But they never listened to me; their response was to take away my mind and clear thinking with drugs. I couldn't function, I couldn't think.

Please don't judge me for what I have done; for me there was no choice. You have shared my life but there is one thing I could never share with you, until now. Before I tell you what that is I must tell you how I came to that terrible point in my life. The double life I was leading.

Losing the love of my life broke me in two. George was a good husband and father. His faith, I have no doubt, was the most important thing in his life but that made him even more special to me and I loved him more for it.

Every day we shared, I knelt and prayed to God giving thanks for my George. I wonder now if he ever knew how much I loved him. Time had made us content and I truly believed we'd be together for the rest of time.

I found it so hard to accept that he would give up. He gave up not only his family, but also his faith. For what? That young girl?

He walked out on his family and his God; breaking Louise's heart as he went.

I worked hard to build a new life for Louise and me but somehow I let her down. I didn't take care of her when she needed me most. I lost sight of what was important. I didn't even notice when she was sad and lonely. What type of mother did I become Madge?

When I realised there was something going on between Alex Turner and my Louise I found it hard to deal with. So I didn't. I thought that, if I ignored it, then perhaps it would run its course and end naturally. I prayed for guidance and the silence seemed to be my sign or did my God desert me?

At first I ignored the obvious, the pattern when Louise would be late home from school. So young and full of hope, I could see myself in her. She would burst in through the kitchen door; smiling, flushed cheeks and explaining that she had called in to see Alex for some reason or another. So many excuses. So many lies. I began to despise him.

When Alex and Susannah announced their pregnancy it was as if a light had been switched off in Louise's heart and I still didn't say anything. This is the end, I thought, she'll never see him again.

That afternoon when Louise came home late from school, I could see she'd been crying. She made some excuse that she was tired and wasn't hungry. She went to her room. She had

been working so hard for her 'A' level exams which made her behaviour plausible; but deep down I knew differently. I believed he had ended their relationship and tossed her to one side. Her heart had been broken just as George had broken mine. I'd never felt such hatred toward another human being as I felt for Alex Turner.

It must have been after nine o'clock when I went up to her room with a sandwich and hot chocolate, her favourite. She had fallen asleep, the light was on and her books were scattered over the bed around her. I sat next to her and stoked her cheeks; they were wet with tears and her eyes red from crying for so long. I felt such anger that my whole body burned with rage. I put her books onto the bedside table, pulled the duvet around her cool body and switched off the light. I can't remember the walk to Jasmine Cottage but I remember walking through the gate and towards the front door. I heard shouting. I went around the back and looked through the French doors. There I saw Susannah and Alex having an almighty row.

I heard her call him a deceitful adulterer.

'I can't believe you could sleep with that child; she's fat, ugly and pathetic.' She screamed at him.

I thought my head would explode with anger.

Alex seemed to lose control. He yelled back at

Susannah but I couldn't understand what he said. He ran to a cupboard in frenzy. It must have been some sort of gun cupboard because he took out a hand gun and pointed it at Susannah.

'Go on! Kill me! Kill me and Philip's child!' Susannah voice was high pitched and vindictive.

Alex dropped the gun in shock. Susannah moved quickly running to kick

the gun away from him. He grabbed her and they wrestled on the floor, screaming at each other. I've never seen such anger and hatred as they lashed out. Scratching and kicking like animals.

They stopped and lay together breathless and exhausted. Alex told her to get out of the house and never come back. Without another word the shaken Susannah obeyed and left the house through the back door. Alex lay on the floor for what seemed ages. I decided to let myself in through the unlocked kitchen door and went into the living room where Alex lay whimpering. I saw the gun where Susannah had kicked it and ran to it snatching it up and pointing it at him before he knew what was happening.

My anger subsided and I felt such power. Those high imperious thoughts now punish me. I can't begin to understand the emotions I felt that night. A feeling of serenity; I had complete control. I think I even smiled as he pleaded in terror and expectation of what this mad woman before him was capable of doing. Words were not necessary. The look on his face told me that he knew. It was now clear to him that I knew everything.

I stood calmly and waited. Alex got to his feet. I could see his body shaking.

I've heard people say they've had out-of-body experiences and until now I didn't know what that meant. I do now.

I spoke but a few words.

'You made her love you. You told her lies, odious, dammed lies.' I growled the words as if from demons within.

There was no time for a response, if indeed he had the asperity to offer one.

I heard the gun go off once, twice, three times and each bullet hit Alex Turner; the man that broke my little girls heart.

I stood alone with Alex's still body just feet away. I was transfixed as I watched his blood soak into the carpet. I

had never seen so much blood, red and thick as it floated onto the carpet and sunk into the pile. I wiped my fingerprints off the gun and put it in his hand. A silly thing to do on reflection but I really didn't have a plan.

You know the rest Madge. The doctors' assumption that I had lost my mind was pretty accurate. The tablets certainly helped. Days drifted from one to another and now my Louise is locked up for a murder I committed. I have to save Louise from any more pain.

Please, Madge, free my girl.

I know you'll go into the greenhouses and will find this letter so the only thing left is for you to give it to the police and Louise can be set free.

The house is paid for and there is money in the bank. Maybe she will continue with my orchid growing and live a good, long life. I hope she will find the right man for herself and marry; maybe even have children. That's something I would have loved to see.

One last thing my friend. Please try to find George; Louise will need him now more than ever.

You may wonder why I placed this letter against my beautiful orchid. At my darkest moments the beauty of this

wonderful flower would raise my spirit. It may be just a black orchid to many but to me it's much, much more.

It gave me and Louise the freedom of a good, secure life. It's paid our bills when I had nothing and it gave me a purpose. Apart from Louise the orchid is the most beautiful thing in

my life. When she is released there is enough money to get her settled until she decides what she wants to do for the rest of her life. Be there for her Madge.

Tell her I will love her forever though we'll not see each other for a while. One day we'll be together again. Her dad always called this orchid the black one and perhaps on this occasion that name is a more fitting one. I smile as I think of dear George, I wish I had been a better wife to him and maybe he would have loved me more. I have to forgive him now for the pain he caused; I hope to meet my maker with love in my heart not hatred. There has been such pain and sadness in my life, I'm so very weary.

I pray that God will forgive my sins and take me to his side.

I want you to know that I trust only you with a letter such as this and pray that if I am taken into heaven and forgiven for my sins I will see you one day. I am and always will be grateful for your friendship Madge. Life is a strange truth. For the first time in my life I am drinking alcohol. I read somewhere that alcohol lessens the fear when you take your own life. I have taken half the amount of drugs needed to end my pain and will take the rest after I have placed this letter for you to find. Then I will enjoy a silent sleep; at peace once more.

Remember this:-

'Moderate lamentation is the right of the dead: excessive grief is the enemy of the living'.

Your friend in this world and the next. God bless you Madge.

Daphne

George folded the letter once, twice, three times as if the importance of the words would lessen or even disappear. He gripped it tightly in the palm of his hand until it became invisible from his sight. But he felt it still.

His sadness was too great for tears. He sat and sat, holding the words in his hand, in his heart, tearing at his very soul. The beat of his heart felt like syncopated explosions. His chest heaved uncontrollably.

The paper was damp and old but the words had been clear. What wasn't clear to George was what he should do next...............